LONDON

Smoke, Blokes and Jokes
of Foggy Town

WADDLE THE WORLD WITH RED PENGUIN BOOKS

London

Copyright © 2022 by Stephanie Larkin

Published by Red Penguin Books

Bellerose Village, New York

ISBN

Print 978-1-63777-314-7

Digital 978-1-63777-315-4

CONTENTS

MEET OUR CONTRIBUTORS

Primrose
Hill

Old Mother
Red Caps

a *PARIS* chez
le Rouge rue des g.ds
Augustins

1

Fig Lane

PANCRAS

ILINGTO

The Buel

O

N

500   1000 Toises

Battle
Bridge

Dagels
Farm

L

River
Pond

Pan
q

MARYLE BONE

TOTTENHAM COURT

CONDUIT

Blacks Marys Well

2

LAMB'S   FIELDS

Foundling
H.sp.

112 113

Tile
Kiln

Hyde

3

PARK

Cupers
Garden
Stairs

Knights
Bridge

LAMBETH

Pont de
Westmin-
ter

St GEORG

4

PIMLICO

FIELDS

Bloody
Bridge

S   O

TOTTHILL
FIELDS

5

PART ONE
LONDON PROPER

PIGEON HEROES

VALERIE ORMOND

Big Ben tolled its bells for the first time in four years at midnight on New Year's Eve, 2022, following refurbishment and scaffolding.

The call to arms brought pigeons flocking back their tower clock home. A steel bird cage had ensnared their home in a contraption they didn't understand with no warning for years. Now, the birds drowned out the tolling bells as they cried for distant cousins across England, Scotland, Ireland, and Wales to join them and rejoice in their return to their brick nest. The feathered prophets from across the United Kingdom heeded the call, and before daylight a multi-colored swarm surrounded the spire in formation. They cooed in harmony for the freedom of their home and hoped the world would hear their song.

The pigeon leader, Paddy, was pleased with the outcome. But he had been thinking hard during Big

Ben's reconstruction, which had displaced much of his former flock. Paddy knew his newly created flock could do something bigger than sing and swarm. He assembled the birds in the stone plaza where he could address them all at once.

"I thank you for joining the successful return to our cherished Big Ben. I welcome back the old members of my flock and welcome the newcomers from across our lands. It was important we took a stand and let the people of Great Britain know we have a voice. As you know, we are the most unappreciated bird in history," Paddy said, strutting back and forth in front of the group.

The crowd shouted cries of support and bobbed their heads.

"And today, we have a chance to let people know who we are, who are ancestors have been, and the contributions we've made in war and keeping this nation, and other nations, free."

"Yes, yes!" a dark pigeon, Blackie said, raising a wing. "But how do you suppose we'll do that, Paddy?"

"I have a plan," Paddy announced. "It will take all of us. Some of us have homes, with owners, fanciers, or masters. Others of us have street skills, and long distance flying skills. But here is something I don't know: can any bird here write?"

A hush fell over the assembly. Birds looked left and right, blinking at each other. A small hen spoke up in a soft voice, looking down; "I can write. But no one is supposed to know. My master who taught me said birds would think I was cursed, and humans would try to take me away if anyone found out."

"So then why do you trust us?" Paddy asked.

"Because I've never seen anything like what I saw today! We came together from across our kingdom. We stood strong. We showed people we are a powerful bird with something to say!"

"And what is your name, wee one?" Paddy asked.

"Mary, sir, named after the famous Mary Poppins. My master said he could tell I was magical from the start. I don't think I'm magical. I think all pigeons could learn to write if we learned and had the right tools."

"How do we know this crazy chick can write?" a rough disbeliever mocked with a thick Cockney accent. Paddy's bright red eyes blazed through the troublemaker Paddy knew as Spike. The cock stepped back from the fiery challenge.

An older hen chirped, "Be careful how you speak about my daughter, you old coot." She moved closer to Mary and swung her protective wing around her.

"Stop!" Paddy ordered. "We need to work together to make this happen. We are smart as a species, so I suspected at least one of us would have learned to write by now. Thank you, Mary, for sharing your special powers with us at great personal risk to yourself. And don't you worry, no one here will hurt you." He glared at the rude Spike.

The flock' low-throated coos echoed in support.

"Okay, let's move on and talk about the plan. Many of you out there have stories from your family histories. We need to share these stories. We are going to tell the world about Cher Ami, GI Joe, and the many other homing pigeons that have braved battles and saved lives," Paddy said.

"I have stories to tell passed down by me American cousins!" a middle-aged hen shouted with an Irish brogue. "Let's get started!"

"Mary, are you willing to write these stories? And can you trust your master enough to share our plan with him?" Paddy asked.

"Of course she will, Paddy," Mary's mother, Ruby, said for her. "And our master has raised our families for generations and has recognized our intelligence. If this mission is important, he will support us."

Paddy said, "And one more thing, if Mary writes the stories, we will need your master's help to get these stories printed so we can distribute them. If we don't have that support, our plan won't work."

Mary said, "We'll go ask, but he will help us. He tells me all the time that people don't know what we've done. Mr. Paddy, are you sure you don't know our master, because you sound a lot like him?" She cocked her head to the side, and her beak parted in a smile.

Paddy sighed and shook his head. "No, young lady, I am not a human in a pigeon's body, but your master sounds like a wise man. Why don't you and your mother–

and father, if he's here–go check and see if we can secure the assistance we need. Let's all meet back here at first light tomorrow morning and discuss on our next steps."

A cock named Winston said, "Let's go," and the pigeon family of three took flight to the west. Others squawked and cooed and shared stories that they hoped the mysterious writing hen would record. Others gossiped that the whole idea was implausible and suggested maybe Paddy was losing his marbles with his age. Eventually, the birds parted their ways for the evening.

Day light arrived, and Mary, Ruby, and Winston flew in, met by the awaiting Paddy. Moments later, close to one hundred pigeons that had gathered the day before collected again in the plaza greeting each other in rolling chirps. Paddy met first with Mary's family speaking in hushed tones before breaking the news to his flock.

"We have good news! Mr. Watson, the master, has agreed to support our mission. Let's hear a cheer of support for Mary and her family for daring to ask a human for help in telling our stories."

The birds stomped their tiny feet and cooed in approval. Enthusiastic pigeons took flight and performed aerial acrobatics.

Winston spoke, "There's one condition, though. Mary's powers must be kept a secret. We don't want her to be in danger, and Mr. Watson is adamant in protecting her. We must have everyone's agreement to secrecy to move forward."

The leader took charge; "We'll swear an oath, then. Flock, repeat after me, we will not divulge how we accomplished our mission…"

The bird chorus recited the oath, some raising their right wings for effect.

"Nor will we disclose Mary's powers outside this group, so help me God."

They completed the oath, nodding in agreement as a team.

"Here is the final plan: Mary will write the stories you would like to tell. They can be stories passed down from your family or stories you know to be true. Be as concise as possible because we want people to read them – no more than three sentences, please. We will start with the section to the left of me," Paddy said, looking out at the crowd, "and work to the right. Those who don't have a story to tell, please rest up and join us tomorrow, at dawn again. We still have jobs for you." He blinked and nodded in affirmation.

Half of the birds departed, and Mr. Watson arrived with Mary's custom keyboard. He developed the keyboard so she could use her toes, bill, and wing tips to type, making her quite fast. He beamed as she demonstrated her skills to her onlookers.

Paddy assisted Mary in gathering the birds' stories. A few were lavish and needed to be condensed, and some were merely ten words. Mary had never written so much. Her toes cramped from punching the keyboard. Her wings ached from overuse in this unnatural position for a pigeon. Her neck tired from continued pecking. But she didn't want to let her family, her master, and her new flock leader down, so she kept working.

Mr. Watson saw Mary's fatigue and said, "little one, I wish I could help. But you are the only pigeon I can communicate with, so I have no idea what your flock mates are saying. I hate to see you like this and feel helpless, like I should have never agreed to this idea. Maybe I can help type for you on a human keyboard if you tell me their stories?"

"No, you don't understand! This is the most important thing I've done in my life! This is why I have special powers, and this is why you taught me to write. I am indebted to you forever for giving me the ability to share my species' contributions about how we have made a difference."

By the end of the day, Mary produced thirty stories of amazing pigeon feats. She also sprinkled in fun facts she thought would interest the general public. Mr. Watson praised her for her creativity and for her thinking of her "audience." Her short leaflet stories included:

• During WWI, when Cher Ami departed on what would be her most important flight, she was immediately shot down resulting in chest and eye wounds and almost severing her leg. She got back up, and due to her tenacity, delivered her message and helped save 194 soldiers of the "Lost Battalion."

• Did you know pigeons' average flying speed is 97 kilometers an hour? And pigeons can fly great distances of up to 1,800 kilometers.

• G.I. Joe was the first American winner of Britain's Dickin Medal for Gallantry for saving at least 100 lives during a WWII battle. He flew 20 miles in only 20 minutes to deliver the message just in time to stop a bombing mission which would have killed and injured Allied soldiers.

• Pigeons mate for life, and both the mother and father take time sitting on the eggs during incubation. Pigeons understand equality!

• Pigeons served on warships carrying important messages from ship to shore, and Navy pilots carried pigeons aboard seaplanes while patrolling for submarines during WWI.

• Thirty-two pigeons received the Dickin Medal for Gallantry for brave service during war including Winkie, Tyke, White Vision, Commando, G.I. Joe, Royal Blue, and William of Orange. Pigeons are war heroes!.

• Columbidae bird family members Cher Ami and G.I. Joe were among the first recipients of the American Animals in War & Peace Medal of Bravery for their valiant lifesaving efforts during two world wars.

• • •

Paddy gathered the flock the day of the final mission and paraded in front of them. "We have done it! First, we got Big Ben back after a long wait, and now, our more important mission. We share our stories with London, and those stories will spread throughout the world."

He instructed the flock. "Here, we have the stack of printed leaflets, thanks to you all for your stories. A big thank you goes to Mary for her tireless writing, and for her ability to communicate with Mr. Watson to request his help to have these printed. Well, and of course to Mr. Watson for supporting our cause."

Blackie interrupted, "And how about you? We could not have done this without you, Paddy. Let's hear it for our leader!"

The flock cooed and bobbed their heads in support, flapped their wings, stomped their feet, and showed their support and admiration for their leader.

Paddy looked down, cleared his throat, and continued, "Every bird will take part by picking up flyers and distributing them by air throughout our great city and beyond. Not only will we be doing a great service to our breed, but we will surely create interest by this mystery. We, our ancestors, and pigeons worldwide will finally be appreciated for the intelligent and brave birds we are. Now go forth and carry out the plan of the day!"

News of the leaflets traveled faster than the speed of pigeons' flight. The mystery intrigued people. How did the birds get the leaflets? And how did they know people needed to know the stories? The story broke on all London media outlets with commentators speculating on theories including that the bird fanciers had cooked up the idea as a publicity stunt. The bird fanciers quickly denied that and jokingly said that pigeons were smart enough to figure out how to do it themselves. Little did they know.

Before long, the pigeon leaflet mystery news spread throughout the globe. The flock had accomplished its mission, and 100 birds working as a team with a strong leader, a special hen, and a supportive human made history. Pigeons reminded humanity of the special birds they were, and their special mission helped people recognize their talents and remember their brave and selfless contributions to preserving freedom and democracy.

GETTING LOST IN LONDON

AMBER PRIMDAHL

On my first trip to London, I realized just how easy it is to get around, and that my anxiety about learning how to use the transit system was unnecessary. This made exploring really fun because I didn't have to worry much about getting lost since the transit lines make it easy to find your way again.

I decided to take the day before returning home to let myself just wander to my heart's content. I took the tube to the Covent Garden stop and got off. It was still pretty early in the morning when I first arrived, so there weren't huge crowds around as I began to browse the shops and stalls in the area.

After some shopping, I just began to wander on the surrounding streets, mostly marveling at the stunning architecture around me. With my camera in hand, I took random streets until I really had no clue where I was. It was such a beautiful, sunny, spring day, and it was getting close to lunchtime, so I wanted to look for a place to grab a quick bite to eat. I found a small place on a random corner and grabbed a sandwich, and continued onwards, looking for a nice place to sit with my meal.

As I kept walking, I found a long street that was lined with Union Jack flags, and it turned out I had stumbled across The Mall, which leads up to Buckingham Palace. Ironically, with such a limited schedule on this trip, I had decided against visiting Buckingham Palace, but since it was in front of me now, I was looking forward to getting up close to see it for myself. However, before I ventured down The Mall, I crossed the street to walk through St. James Park. This was definitely a great atmosphere to have my lunch and to take a bit of a walking break.

I wandered through the park where they were by chance having a big event there that day, so on top of the beautiful nature to be seen, there were also a lot of military vehicles to see too. After looking around for a while, I sat on a bench and people watched while I ate my lunch, then carried on towards Buckingham Palace.

Seeing Buckingham Palace was definitely a fun experience. As a history buff, I love to know that I am standing in a place that holds so much history. There were, of course, huge crowds all around the Palace, selfie sticks and all, so I grabbed a few of my photos and continued on to the gift store to buy a little souvenir for my mom. A few days before my visit, Princess Charlotte had been born, so I bought my mom a pencil with a little princess sitting on the top, which she still has in her office to this day.

From here, I continued to walk around the neighborhood until I felt I was ready to go back to my accommodation and rest my weary feet. I hopped on a nearby tube and easily returned to where I began.

When you give yourself time just to wander, you never know what you'll come across, and it's a great way to see some new places in the city you're traveling to. I wouldn't have seen any of this outside of my planned Covent Garden stop if I had tried to create a rigid plan for the day, and it turned out to be my favourite day that I spent in London on that trip.

Chestnut Roasting

Mark Andrew Heathcote

Chestnut roasting on an autumn night
or in a roasting pan,
lit by a tardy London streetlight.

Chestnuts roasting come, buy, come buy
chestnuts roasting sold to a serviceman;
something truly earthly he can quantify.

Chestnut roasting, placed into a paper bag.
Chestnut roasting, nothing like them "chum!"
Come, buy them, oh come and buy them by the kilogram.

Chestnut roasting on an autumn night
chestnut roasting under the moonlight
chestnuts roasting come and eat some "tonight!"

The Last Voyage of The Fighting Temeraire

Dany Gagnon

I can still see myself a teenager running
to the National Gallery at lunch time
to sit and stare tears welling at this effusion of colours
I was in love with Turner with The Fighting Temeraire
in love with the whirlwind of blending hues
I saw beauty glory in the golden shades

I did not see death nor the scavengers awaiting
the end of a proud fighting life replaced by a new era -
fifty years later all I see is the old woman
my mind can no longer decode the young lady
in the optical illusion that is our lives
we see with our fears our memories and our aches

a magnificent boat towed to its last berth
an aging body disappearing in a blazing sunset
a mixed of beauty demise and impending death

Turner was my age when he painted this last voyage
did he also feel the waning of greatness
did he see beauty born out of sinking sadness

DARKNESS BEFORE DAWN

DONNA KEEL ARMER

Never in the field of human conflict was so much owned by so many to so few ~ Winston Churchill

We are neither ducks or Londoners—

Today delivers the visual image I have of London—wet, chilly, gray—perfectly London. Ensconced in rain jackets, we cross from Westminster to Pimlico. The only redeeming elements are the big hanging baskets of flowers brightening a listless day.

Pimlico is charming—little shops, restaurants, cafes, and people—friendly and courteous. They nod politely when we bang their umbrellas with ours. They stop their cars to let us cross the street. By late afternoon, the sun is out. But in the few days we've been here, we understand hooded raincoats and/or umbrellas are a daily necessity in London.

Skipping over the puddles, we make our way to Grumbles—what's in a name? It turns out plenty. The restaurant opened in 1964. They still brag about having the same decor and furniture as when it opened. Perhaps an omen?

We have reservations for a traditional London meal in this tiny hole-in-the-wall restaurant.

There are six tables, three booths, and three outside tables. The tables outside drip forlornly in the damp air as we push open the heavy wooden door. We are seated at a small table in the corner with a view of both the door and the entire restaurant.

We do not have high expectations for the food as friends have warned us that English food will not suit our culinary tastes. Still, we check out the charm, the hospitality, and the service. All are at a pleasing level. How could the food be bad?

The restaurant fills up quickly. There are exuberant greetings and hugs are exchanged between the staff and their regular customers. The table closest to the door is occupied by a woman alone who is content to eat her meal and read her e-book.

An elderly gentleman limps through the door. He's noticeable with his cane which he leans on heavily while catching his breath. He explains to the hostess he doesn't have a reservation. Perhaps there's a small spot he can squeeze into.

The hostess sighs, frowns, and purses her mouth as she, after carefully examining the seating area, tells him there's no room. He nods and shuffles toward the door with slumped shoulders. Just as he places his hand on the knob, the woman sitting alone says, "Please sit with me, that's if you don't mind company."

The sweet invitation lights up his face. His smile spreads until it spills out of his eyes. "Don't mind if I do," he says.

A lovely conversation ensues between young and old. We eavesdrop on their histories and storytelling.

Our food arrives to deadly silence. Ray and I consider ourselves to be overly involved with gastronomy. In our past history, we owned a restaurant and catering service, so we feel obligated to assess food from all directions of smell, taste, texture, and visual presentation as well as cultural and historical significance.

Ray's appetizer is a thimble-sized sliver of smoked mackerel on a few limp greens topped by three pieces of whitish chopped tomato. My shrimp cocktail is white— both the miniature shrimp and the overflowing glop of what turns out to be mayonnaise sauce. It's served in a glass bowl that fits into the palm of my hand.

He tentatively pokes at the mackerel and declares what little there is, although low on presentation, has quite a solid smoky taste. My shrimp cocktail misses the mark completely. It's easily summed up as bland and mushy. Oh, for a sprig of parsley.

The main course arrives. It's a handsome plate. We nod in appreciation as we eyeball the thick slab of rare roast beef, the roasted parsnips, and stewed cabbage with carrots. On top of the hearty fare is a steaming Yorkshire pudding, soaking in beef gravy.

Ray has a cardinal rule to never add salt to any food he's served. He reasons it's the chef's responsibility to perfectly flavor the food, not the customer's. First, he tries to cut the slab of beef, which remains uncuttable. He moves to the parsnips. After the first bite, he reaches for the salt shaker.

I continue to see-saw on the beef. It looks so appealing until my teeth clamp into the tough, stringy meat. It refuses to move. I chew for a very long time. That was my first and last bite. Ray continues to add salt to the meat, to the parsnips, and to the cabbage and carrots. He declares the Yorkshire pudding the only eatable ingredient on his plate. Our saving grace is that the Bordeaux we ordered to accompany our meal is excellent.

Yes, the food was a failure, but we loved the cheery atmosphere and the experience. We have now eaten

English food. We will not do it again. But we did find wonderful ethnic restaurants—Spanish, Italian, and Turkish during our stay. But what we did find in that tiny restaurant transcends food—it was, above all, a community, a place where everybody knows your name.

As we leave the restaurant, the sun tips its hat to us. The hanging baskets come to life, nodding their great bursts of color in the breeze. I check to ensure I have the tickets I pre-ordered online for Churchill's War Rooms before we walk the long way on Buckingham Palace Road. We have time, and it's worth a glimpse of the Palace and a walk through St. James Park. It's a pleasant burst of green surrounded by traffic. It overflows with locals and tourists out for a Sunday stroll.

We have limited time in London before heading to Ireland. Our list is short: Westminster Abbey, Buckingham Palace and the Queen's State Rooms, and Churchill's War Rooms. Having advanced tickets takes us to the front of the line. We are ushered in only to discover the rooms are packed with tourists. My biggest difficulty when traveling is I always long for a leisurely stroll through famous places instead of being swept along with the herd. Often my wish is granted, but not today.

Winston Leonard Spencer-Churchill (1874-1965) was born to an American mother and English father. He was a great man, a soldier, a politician, and a writer—a man of great courage and tenacity.

The Churchill War Rooms were created as an underground bunker that allowed Britain's leaders to plot the allied route to victory during WWII. Construction of the War Rooms began in 1938. They became fully operational on August 27, 1939, a week before Britain declared war on Germany. These rooms remained in operation until the surrender of Japan in August 1945.

At first, I think the crowds make it difficult to understand what it must have been like to live underground for the duration of the war. But as elbows graze my back and the air hangs heavy, I realize I'm experiencing a good example of poor ventilation. It isn't adequate for the number of tourists jammed into the small rooms. I close my eyes and visualize what it would have felt like to live underground for six years with poor ventilation, no windows, and no light. I'm a person of light. I cannot survive without it. Shivers slide down my spine. I marvel at those who rose to the occasion.

The bedrooms are broom-closet size, complete with a cot, a desk, a chamber pot, a telephone, and one lamp. Although both Churchill and his wife had bedrooms at the War Rooms, they rarely slept there. Churchill wanted to be at 10 Downing Street. His wish was to be visible to the citizens as much as possible.

During its operational life, the two most important rooms were the Map Room and the Cabinet Room. The Map Room was in constant use and manned around the clock by officers of the Royal Navy, British Army, and the Royal Air Force. These officers were responsible for producing a daily intelligence report for the King, the Prime Minister, and the military Chiefs of Staff.

The Cabinet Room wasn't utilized until Winston Churchill was appointed Prime Minister. He designated the room as the place where he would direct the war. One hundred fifteen Cabinet meetings were held in the room, with the last one on March 28, 1945, when the German V-weapon bombing campaign ended.

I was 20 when Churchill died. I remember watching the pageantry on TV and thinking what a remarkable person he was—the right man for the job—certainly the right man to save Great Britain and alert the rest of the world. Early on, he recognized the threat Hitler posed and sent out the alarm to Britain's allies.

Today, I again watched the film of his funeral. I notice the facial expressions on those gathered—the great sadness, the salute of a child, the bowed head of a soldier, and the military pallbearers straining as they mount the numerous steps to St. Paul's cathedral, thousands in attendance. The only sounds—the click of the soldiers' heels, the soft thud of the horses' hooves, the gun salute. I am forever grateful for this man.

We take the short way back to the apartment. We pick our way through endless traffic (cars and people). Fumes of double-decker buses assault us, and protestors wave banners in our faces and beat drums as they rage against some real or perceived error, usually on the part of the government.

The door closes with a thud. We open the draperies to our view over Kings Scholar Passage in Westminster. Without speaking, Ray produces a bottle of Primitivo wine and two glasses. I pilfer the fridge for cheeses, olives, and spicy sausages. To the tray, I add the crusty bread we picked up at the market on the way back.

Ray pours the rich, robust wine. We swivel our chairs to the view and raise our glasses, "To Churchill!"

We make a living by what we get, but we make a life by what we give ~ Winston Churchill

TOM FELTON & AN INCONVENIENT QUEEN

ELAINE GILMARTIN

You would think with all the hype surrounding Queen Elizabeth II's 70th Jubilee, one would be aware, but evidently not us. Eager to visit our daughter in London, my husband and I booked a trip to visit the beginning of June according to her work schedule.

I've got a few days off, bank holiday, she had declared.

Great, see you then!

Of course as the date for our trip neared, we couldn't miss the hype surrounding the Queen's celebration. Anticipation for the Jubilee was plastered all over the news. So we fervently hoped she wouldn't, um, you know, go to that big throne in the sky until after our trip as that would shut everything in London down.

As luck would have it, that sturdy old broad just kept chugging, so London would be wide open for us to enjoy at our leisure.

Leisure? Did I write leisure?

Good thing I am a New Yorker accustomed to pushing my way down Seventh Avenue to race for a train out of Penn Station, because crowded does not begin to describe it!

As this was my husband's first time in London, my fifth, my daughter and I wanted to show him the typical tourist sites.

Buckingham Palace...um, no, apparently ten thousand other people had the same idea...

See honey, that speck on the horizon? That's the palace!

London Eye? Nope, closed for the Jubilee weekend.

Look up, honey, do you see how that could have been fun?

Going out to dinner proved its own challenge. The wonderful Sky Garden Restaurant my daughter and I enjoyed the year before was booked solid.

See that really tall building, honey? Way up top with all the windows is the restaurant with the yummy sweet potato gnocchi and the spectacular view overlooking the Thames!

Okay, okay, so it was challenging and it was crowded, but it was London after all with its rich history and scenic parks and endless pubs. So much to do and enjoy and my husband isn't the biggest fan of heights anyway.

With our hotel located right across from Battersea Park, we began each day sitting by the duck pond, coffee in hand, discussing the day's itinerary. That in itself was a joy, relishing this time with our daughter, hearing about her exploits in this great city, her enthusiasm for work in the field of international justice readily evident.

Our first foray was a tour of the Winston Churchill War Rooms, which was not only educational, but also allowed me to channel my inner Winston and do a few impersonations.

We shall fight on the beaches...we shall fight in the streets...we shall fight in the hills...we shall never surrender!

My daughter just rolled her eyes.

The Sherlock Holmes Museum proved fascinating as we wend our way through the four floors of mystery and intrigue, although my exclamations of *Elementary, my dear Watson* got tired fast.

And boy, did we walk, one day as much as thirty thousand steps. Half of them just to get to a restaurant able to seat us. But the weather was perfect and we did see so much.

The one fortunate thing my daughter and I did was to buy tickets in advance for a show at the Tower of London called, "The Gunpowder Plot." My daughter being twenty-three years old and weaned on Harry Potter was a fan of the series, so when she heard the actor, Tom Felton, who played Draco Malfoy, would be the featured star, it was a no-brainer.

Sending me the link to buy the tickets weeks before we arrived, my daughter explained it would be half virtual, half live performance with audience participation. Never one to say no to anything remotely intriguing, I checked the dates, number of tickets available for our time there, and saw some discrepancy with the prices. Thinking the more expensive ones included a buffet afterwards, I selected the cheaper ones and hit submit.

We surprised my husband that day with the plan. And after the daily refrain of, *Oh that would have been nice but...*, he was thrilled.

You mean they can't turn us away? He asked, incredulous look on his face.

Nope, we are booked!

After our morning coffee at the pond, as had become our custom those several days, we strolled through Borough Market, my daughter pointing out the building used in the iconic *Bridget Jones Diary* scene. We bought some souvenirs at a nearby street fair and then made our way to the Tower of London.

That is, the three of us, along with thousands upon thousands of other people, converged on this busy tourist spot. Combined with an uncharacteristically high temperature and intense sun, we were all getting a little testy.

At the entryway, our tickets were scanned and once admitted, we were directed to the lower level.

As we descended the stairs into the dark abyss, the temperature dropped and our eyes had to adjust to the sudden gloom. Fog added to the atmosphere and a sense of anticipation renewed our spirits and energy.

And as we gathered with several other visitors, a guide informed us the actors would all be in character and we would interact with them directly. My husband gave me a sideways glance, basically conveying a, *What the hell did you get me into?* look. I ignored him.

Once inside, we were provided a brief history lesson on The Gunpowder Plot. I will admit I do not recall hearing this bit of English history, but having previously toured the Tower of London, I was well aware Protestants and Catholics were at direct odds since Elizabeth I instituted Protestantism as the national religion after her notorious father, Henry the VIII, converted when he got an answer he didn't like. Basically, you can't divorce your wife. That was it for Catholicism.

So Catholics caught in the act of clandestine religious services were imprisoned, tortured, executed, you know, all the fun stuff from that era.

After Elizabeth dies in 1603, her cousin James of Scotland assumes the throne. The persecution did not relent so on November 5 1605, a plot to ignite barrels of gunpowder underneath Parliament to assassinate King James I was planned, hence, The Gunpowder Plot.

As you would rightly guess, this plan was foiled and one of the conspirators, Guy Fawkes, was captured, imprisoned in the Tower of London and after being tortured for weeks, gave up the names of his co-conspirators, who, along with Fawkes, were executed. And now we would get to relive that. Oh goodie.

Ushered into a darkened room out of a movie set, the ten of us stood there meeting one another's eyes in the gloom, a family of four with two pre-teens, a young couple, a solo woman-kudos-and the three of us.

I was about to whisper something sarcastic to my daughter about the lighting when in burst a man from a door I hadn't noticed. Taking in his appearance, I would have to say he struck me as a clone of Orlando Bloom from Pirates of the Caribbean, that is if he had a beard, all swashbuckling and frankly, *hot*, and I nudged my daughter in his direction.

Go on, interact.

Well acquainted with my sense of humor, she glared back at me when *Orlando* commanded us to put on the cloaks hanging behind us on the wall, telling us we must hurry as the British forces would soon be onto us.

We did so hurriedly as I whispered to my daughter, *Is that Tom Felton?*

She shook her head vigorously as we took off after Orlando, who, to my defense, could have been Tom given the beard and poor lighting.

Running through a dark and narrow passageway, I thought maybe I should have paid more attention when they explained why we could have no personal items or phones with us. I thought it was simply to get into the spirit of the times, not safety as we navigated low ceilings and random rafters in our path.

Entreating my husband to open a heavy wooden door, Orlando commanded us onward and then to sit on wooden swings.

Ooo a ride, I cried.

Orlando shot that down.

No, you must rescue the priest-he is being tortured in the tower!

Once seated, we were instructed to put on headsets that opened to us a virtual world. I have to say I was impressed. Seeming as if we could simply reach out to the imprisoned man on the floor, we were suddenly airborne, helping to lower him by rope to safety. The sensation of floating on air was compounded by our wooden swings and when told it was time to leave, I hesitated.

But this is fun!

My daughter pushed me along.

Running down another passageway, we encountered two additional characters, a man and a woman in character and costume. The man was evidently not Tom.

When are we going to see Tom?

My daughter shrugged.

And on we went, placed in jail at one point, released and allowed a brief respite for drinks and restrooms-not very character-y, I thought, although I did appreciate not having to resort to using a hole in the floor.

On we went, the characters spurring us to join Guy Fawkes and light that fuse-and then directing us to climb into lifeboats.

Oh cool-maybe we'll float the rest of the way!

My husband nudged me to put on the virtual headset under our seats. And once again we were immersed in this amazing world where we floated along the Thames, huge boats surrounding us. I actually ducked as one loomed dangerously close. And then in front of us appeared a virtual Guy Fawkes, urging us to row faster as *the time was nigh!*

Well, remaining historically accurate, we were informed the gunpowder was never lit. The final leg of our journey had us surrounded by the buildings and bridges of London, all lit against the night sky as poor Guy Fawkes informed us of his capture, the plot foiled, and now every November 5th England celebrates with fireworks and bonfires and I would imagine a lot of alcohol.

Wait a minute, I declared as we were directed to the exit. *Where's Tom Felton?*

He was Guy Fawkes, my daughter told me, *didn't you recognize him?*

Ah, I should have but I was so taken with the realism of the virtual world that I was fixated on the boats and the Thames and the stars of the night sky. And once we retrieved our phones, I saw the 'cheaper' tickets did not include the Tom Felton meet-n-greet. Oops.

Okay, that could have been fun, but we had had such a good time that ultimately it did not matter. I mean, Tom could have been worth paying almost double the pounds per ticket, but what we experienced was amazing and fun and unforgettable.

Our final night in London had us watching the

Queen on television chat up Paddington Bear virtually; apparently when unable to get a celebrity or royal in person, go virtual. It's the next best thing.

With a morning flight from Heathrow back to New York, we had only limited time with our daughter before saying good-bye. Encapsulating possibly my favorite time, the three of us sat, coffee in hand, by that beautiful duck pond, savoring not so much where we were, but that London had brought us together in ways meaningful and precious, reminding us that an ocean cannot separate what is always in our hearts.

FROM A WINDOW: THE STORY OF PHIL

WILLIAM JOHN ROSTRON

London was abuzz about the city's current athletic events, especially the upcoming race. With all of her children involved in the festivities, Queen Alexandra had taken on the responsibility of amusing her grandchildren. While she could have allowed one of an army of well-trained nannies to put the children to sleep, Queen Alexandria was a grandmother at heart, and liked to look upon their little faces that would eventually take over the country she had given her life to.

"Please tell us the story again," asked Henry, who was 8.

"Again? Don't you ever grow tired of the same tale?"

"No!" they answered in unison Henry continued, "Especially since we shall see it actually happen tomorrow."

"Well, you are not actually going to see it. Tomorrow is just a re-creation…a commemoration of the event," she answered quite calmly, not having the nerve to tell them that there was a very strong possibility that security concerns might keep them from seeing anything at all. The least she could do would be to tell them the story again.

"Yes, grandmother, please tell us of Philepsi… Philoso….Phil…something," begged Olaf, the second youngest at five. English was not his first language—a product of his father's Norwegian birth.

"You know what, Olaf? In the story, we shall call him Phil this time," consented the Queen, also not a native English speaker.

Edward and George, the eldest two, laughed at calling the story's hero "Phil." However, they conceded that most of their younger cousins would never be able to pronounce the Greek legend's name, Pheidippides.

"Yeah, tell us about Phil, grandmother," mocked the two brothers, who would one day both be kings of their country.

"Now, now, boys, if you are ever to rule, you must learn to have compassion for those who do not understand everything you do. Love, compassion, and empathy are just as important as strength, intelligence, and leadership," scolded the Queen.

George smirked at this concept and turned to his brother Edward who stood straight-faced and did not react at first, but then nodded to the older woman.

"I understand," was all Edward would say. Twenty-eight years later, he would abdicate as the king of England after less than a year on the throne—a choice made so that he could pursue the love of a woman who was unacceptable to English royalty.

"If we are all done with the fiddle-faddle, I will relate the story of Phil." She glanced over at the two oldest with a look that challenged them to comment. George made a motion as if zipping his mouth shut. Edward laughed and then imitated him in response. Finally, all the grandchildren sat and listened to their grandmother, Queen Alexandra.

"So once upon a time," she began but was soon interrupted by Mary, who was eleven.

"Grandmother, I didn't know this was a fairy tale?"

"It is not. I'm sorry. Two-thousand-four hundred and eighteen years ago…. Is that better, Mary?"

"Yes, Grandmother."

"The people of Athens were engaged in a great war with the people of Persia. These two countries were neighbors, only separated by a small body of water. However, they had disputes that soon blossomed into a major conflict."

"That could never happen today," interrupted Mary. "This is the 20th century. We have learned better than to have giant wars that kill many people."

"Have we?" retorted her grandmother.

"Of course, there will be no great wars in Europe," spoke George confidently, "Someday I will be the king of England...and Grandmother, you know that my cousins sit on the thrones of Germany, Norway, Romania, Russia, Greece, Sweden, and Spain. This is 1908, not the dark ages."

"Well, sometimes quarrels among family can be the worst of all," responded the Queen.

"Really, Grandmother?" said George, who was now quite interested. "No country you mentioned could rival our power...except maybe Germany. And Willy... excuse me...Kaiser Wilhelm II is my first cousin and friend."

"A world war...what a ridiculous idea," added Edward.

"Well, I hope you are right," conceded the Queen. "And I hope these 1908 Olympics help bring us all together."

"Grandmother, can you please stop talking to George and Edward and tell us the story of Phil?" whined Henry, who was bored with all the political talk.

"Yes, I will do that presently, and I'll not have another word from you two young men," chided the Queen, looking at George and Edward.

In 490 BC, the Persians invaded Greece," started the

Queen only to hear loud booing from the three youngest children.

"Those nasty Persians," added Mary.

"No, the Greeks had started it at Ionia, but that is another whole story," countered the Queen, losing patience. "Children, I want to finish this story before tomorrow morning, so please don't interrupt."

All went silent.

The two armies met on a great field called Marathon. The most significant part of the Greek army was from Athens, with smaller city-states helping out. However, they were vastly outnumbered by the Persians because their most important ally had not arrived at the battlefield. The army from Sparta would have doubled the size of the defending Greeks.

Pheidippedes...sorry, I mean Phil, was sent as a messenger to beseech the Spartans to come. He ran almost a hundred and fifty miles in two days to beg for their help. The Spartans, however, gave an excuse and never came.

Faced with overwhelming odds against them, the Greek general had to be intelligent in devising a battle plan to save the Athenians. First, he positioned his army behind soft, muddy swampland. As a result, the Persians could not ride their horses to attack, causing them to be on foot.

Then, General Miltiades ordered most of his soldiers to the flanks, the sides of the battlefield. The Persians attacked the middle of the army, thinking it small. It was a trap. When they got close to the waiting Greeks, they were attacked from both sides and routed...er...beaten for you younger children.

The Persians retreated, and the Greeks followed them to their boats, killing many of them on the way.

"Ew," complained Mary, who found this part of the story disgusting.

"I tell you all this because I want you to remember that war is not only about glory and victory, but also about death!"

"Grandmother, finish the story," screeched Henry.

"Yes, Grandmother. The next part is my favorite," mumbled Olaf

While all this was going on, the citizens of Athens were terrified. If the Greek army were defeated, they knew the Persians would march to their city and slaughter them. So they waited desperately for word of the battle. Then, finally, Miltiades summoned...er...Phil.

"Please run as fast as possible and tell the people they are safe. They must know of our victory."

Still exhausted from his run to Sparta and back, Phil sacrificed all to get the message to Athens from the battlefield of Marathon. With little thought to his health, he ran as fast as possible for the 26 miles needed. Upon arriving in Athens, he announced to the people, "We win," and promptly died. He had given everything so that the people of the city could know they would live.

And so that is why tomorrow the Olympics

commemorates that moment when one man sacrificed his life for so many others. And that is why the race is 26 miles, recognizing the distance from the battlefield of Marathon to the city of Athens. That is a good thing. Very few remember the details of that long-ago battle, but we all remember Phil's run.

"Oh, Grandmother, I cannot wait to see the race tomorrow," said Mary, and all of the children agreed.

How could she tell them that at that very minute, security concerns were being discussed that would prevent the children from being at the start of the London Marathon?

"But your majesty, there are reports of anarchists and perhaps a new group called Communists in the crowd that could do you family harm," argued the captain of the Royal Guard.

"I understand," replied King Edward VII, pondering the problem at hand.

"However, it would mean so much to the children,your heirs. They would see firsthand the commemoration of the sacrifice that a human being can make for fellow human beings. Isn't this important for them if they are to be the leaders of the world going forward?" questioned Queen Alexandra sitting by her husband's side.

"Yes, but if they don't live long enough to be those leaders, what good is it?" answered the king.

The debate raged on in the early morning as the marathon runners prepared for their race, unaware of the machinations taking place in Windsor Castle. They went through their individual pre-race rituals designed to ensure finishing the grueling 26-mile test. However, it was not quite exactly what they expected. The Queen had found a solution.

As the runners approached the starting line, race officials notified them that they needed to assemble .2 miles further down the road. This coincided with the exact location of the children's rooms in Windsor Castle. Now, the children could gaze from their windows with a birds-eye view of the starting line. Their grandmother, Queen Alexandra, had found a way to safely bring the race to them.

Standardization of events became a priority for the Olympic Committee that year. It was felt that all performances could then be compared from Olympiad to Olympiad. Therefore, all marathons run since the 1908 London Olympics have been exactly 26.2 miles.

In 1914, World War I broke out. It pitted George V of the United Kingdom (who had succeeded his father in Edward VII in 1910) against his first cousin, Kaiser

Wilhelm II of Germany. Eight of the countries involved in the war were ruled by descendants of Queen Victoria, George, and Wilhelm's grandmother and ruler of the United Kingdom from 1837 to 1901.

ALL IN THE FAMILY - WORLD WAR I

King George V
  United Kingdom
  (Victoria's grandson)

Kaiser Wilhelm II
  Germany
  (Victoria's grandson)

Tsar Nicholas I
  Russia
  (husband of Victoria's granddaughter, Alexandra)

King Haakon VII
  Norway
  (husband of Victoria's granddaughter, Maud)

Ferdinand I
  Romania
  (husband of Victoria's granddaughter, Marie)

King Constantine I
Greece
(husband of Victoria's granddaughter, Sophia)

Crown Prince Gustaf Adolf
Sweden
(husband of Victoria's granddaughter, Margaret)

King Alfonso XIII
Spain
(husband of Victoria's granddaughter, Victoria Eugenie)

18th of March

Womens parties in the society. He
a naturist Noa thing ... for
But no now would so she has known to
are the characters that Tould. It is
think hundreds of thousand of woman have
Now replied In my view the
really characters the plot
... short, ... tells
a middle-aged ...
times, named
the family

PEN PALS

DEBBIE DE LOUISE

Before there was email, texting, or other high-tech communication methods, there was the pen-and-paper letter. Receiving one of these missives could bring extreme joy or devastating sorrow. It was through one of these old-fashioned dispatches that Hillary Mary Johnson received both.

Hillary was an only child whose mother had died during childbirth. Her father, Sid, owned his own business in Queens, New York, a deli chain called Sydney's. On some weekends, he'd bring her to his store to show his little girl off to the workers and customers. He would make her a special sandwich of all her favorite meats – liverwurst that melted in her mouth, the rarest roast beef, tender, thin-sliced turkey, and hot pastrami on a seeded fresh roll. It was heaven. Afterwards, they'd walk down the street to Carl's old-fashioned ice cream parlor and have an egg cream or banana split. On those days, with her father smiling across from her and sweet vanilla ice cream melting on her tongue, she didn't miss not having a mother or any close girlfriends. She was a loner, but she was happy that way. As long as she had her dad, she could cope with her classmates calling her a daddy's girl or making fun of the fact that she was chubby, had acne, too long a nose, and wore thick glasses.

Things began to change when Hillary started college. Although she'd won several scholarships and her dad encouraged her to go away to one of the finer schools, she refused, preferring the local university so she could still live at home. She was interested in learning to be a writer, so she enrolled as an English major with a Creative Writing minor. Sid worried it would be hard to find work except as a teacher, but he praised the poetry and prose she shared with him from her classes, and he was proud that she was an editor on the school newspaper.

It was in her junior year that Sid became ill. He cut back his hours at the deli but told her not to worry about her tuition because he had saved enough to see her graduate. She knew he wished for her to find a husband to take care of her and treat her like a princess. After all, he wouldn't be around forever.

Since at 21, Hillary had only had a few dates in her life, she knew she was far from any marriage proposals. Girls were starting to marry later in the late 80's, and some were focusing on careers over marriage and having a family. Still, Hillary was a romantic at heart. If she met a man like her father, she'd do anything to have him as a husband. Many of the stories she wrote were love stories, and she embraced the romantic poets, especially the love sonnets of Elizabeth Barrett Browning. Those English poets knew heartache, but as Shakespeare said in a famous play, "'Tis better to have loved and lost, than never to have loved at all."

Although Hillary's complexion was now clear, she'd lost the baby fat that had plagued her for years, and she'd finally been able to figure out how to insert contact lenses, she still had a hard time expressing herself except through writing.

One day, she came across something that she thought would change her life. She saw an ad in one of the school library's magazines advertising an international pen pal club. She'd never had a pen pal before, but she thought it might be a nice way to make a friend. Even better, she could do it through writing and not the social face-to-face contact which always made her nervous. Hillary jotted down the address and sent a self-addressed, stamped envelope with a money order for a year's participation in the program. She also included a list of countries from which she was interested in corresponding with pen friends. Since she didn't speak any other language but English, she requested England, Canada, and even the United States, and indicated that she'd be willing to write to both females and males from 21 to 25 years of age.

Hillary didn't mention the pen pals to her father. She knew he wouldn't mind, but she still felt uncomfortable telling him, especially if this new endeavor didn't work out as she planned. She thought she'd start receiving responses immediately, but she didn't hear anything for over a month. She was just about to forget the whole thing when a letter arrived from a Miss Clara Burton at Hamptonshire, England. Her father had taken in the mail that day and seen the foreign address and stamp. It was a Saturday, so she was in her room straightening up when he knocked on the door.

"Hillary, there's a letter for you," he called from outside the door.

Her heart began to thud. Her first pen pal letter. She was so excited. She opened the door. "Thank you, Dad," she said, taking the letter he held out for her.

"It's from England. Who do you know in England, Hill?"

"I joined a pen pal club," she explained. "I thought it would be fun to write to people in other countries."

He wasn't upset. "That's a great idea. It's a nice way to learn about other cultures. I've actually been putting money away for an international trip for you when you graduate. I think you need to see the rest of the world before you start working full-time."

"I know money is tight right now, Dad. How could you find the money to save for a trip and also pay my tuition?"

"Where there's a will, there's a way, dear daughter.

You don't spend money like water. You deserve a nice treat for your good grades at school."

"Thank you so much, Dad." She ran to him and hugged him. If this Clara Burton turned out to be a good friend, maybe she could go to England and meet her. After her dad left, she went back to her room, read Clara's letter, which introduced herself and asked for Clara to share some of her own pastimes, and started to write a reply.

Hillary had been writing to Clara for a few months when she received another pen pal letter. It was a simple and very proper letter.

> "Dear Miss Hillary," it began in excellent penmanship compared to Clara's scrawled notes. "It was my pleasure to receive your name from the International Pen Club. My name is Michael Boxwood. I'm 25 years old and live in the city of London. I'm employed as a librarian in the main archives of the British Library. I, too, enjoy reading, especially the English classic poets Dunne, Blake, Byron, Keats, and Shelley. I write poetry, too. I would love to share some with you if you wouldn't mind. What do you like? Please tell me about yourself, your life, family, and interests. I would be honored to be your pen friend.
>
> Very Sincerely Yours,
> Michael Aaron Boxwood

Hillary corresponded with Clara and Michael for

the next few months. Clara's replies were not as frequent or as long as Michael's, but she felt that she'd made two close friends. Sitting at the antique writing desk in her bedroom, she spent hours composing letters to each of them, revealing her innermost thoughts and feelings in a way she never had before, not even to her father. Her life at college became almost secondary to the life she was living through postal mail. In particular, her letters to Michael began to change from polite interest to a deeper connection. He now addressed her as "My dearest Hillary." She signed her letters, "Affectionately Yours, H." He shared some of his poetry with her including a few poems he wrote just for her, and she sent him some of her stories that he praised with words that were both encouraging and sweet.

At the end of April, a few weeks before her college graduation, her father asked her to have a seat in the parlor so that they could talk. She'd been in the middle of composing a letter to Michael, but she put down her pen and went down to join Sid on their tapestry covered couch. He was looking a bit drawn, and her worries about his health returned. She hoped what he had to tell her didn't involve bad news.

She thought he may have read the fear on her face when he turned to her and said, "Don't worry, Hill. This isn't anything bad. I just wanted to remind you about the trip I'm giving you for graduation. I know you'll need to prepare. You'll probably want to buy some new clothes, pick up traveler's checks, and make your packing list."

Although Hillary hadn't forgotten about the trip, it had been pushed aside in her thoughts like everything else besides her pen pal correspondence. "I guess my mind has been a bit preoccupied, father," she said. "But I do recall you promising me a trip for my graduation."

Sid smiled, and it brightened his pale face. "There are so many places to see in the world, Hill. I wish I could afford to send you to them all. I haven't done much traveling in my life, and I regret that." He sighed. "I'll miss you while you're away, but it'll be great to hear your stories when you return."

"So where am I going?" Hillary envisioned the Eiffel Tower or the Leaning Tower of Pisa, places she'd read about and seen on T.V.

"That's up to you, my dear." Sid stood up. "Your graduation is in just a few weeks, so you'll have to make reservations soon."

It hit her then—the one place she could visit where she already had friends, a place where everyone would speak her language, a place where she could meet a special pen pal who might become much more than that. "Dad," she said, a smile slowly taking over her face, "I'd like to go to England."

It was the first time Hillary had flown on an airplane alone. The only other time she'd even flown anywhere was when her dad had taken her to Disney

World in Florida to celebrate her tenth birthday. She was too excited to worry much, though. She had written to both Clara and Michael about her travel plans. Michael was meeting her at Heathrow, while Clara would meet both of them in London that Saturday.

Hillary's dad hugged her as she left the gateway at JFK to board the plane. "Have fun," he said, but she could tell he was nervous about her traveling solo across the ocean. "I'll pick you up here in a week."

Aboard the plane, Hillary kept herself occupied writing in her diary and observing some of her fellow passengers. She imagined the young couple in front of her was honeymooning in England, and she spoke occasionally with the elderly woman next to her who told her she was visiting her grandchildren. She also noticed some children around twelve who were traveling alone. That gave her courage to face the trip by herself.

As the plane set down comfortably on the runway, she noticed the golden sunshine they would disembark in and realized that it was a myth that the sun never shone in England.

Her heart was thudding as she exited the plane and passed through Customs where she had her passport stamped. She scanned the crowds of people gathered in the waiting area holding signs for their loved ones to notice. Would Michael look like she imagined? He'd sent her a photo of himself and also included a written description saying he was 5'8 and of average weight for a man his age.

As she moved through the crowd after Beverly, her companion from the plane, had joined her family–her daughter and two tow-headed boys who ran to grandma, Hillary noticed a man wearing sunglasses standing beyond the throng holding a poster with bright red letters that read, "Welcome, Hillary!" She excused herself as she made her way around people to reach him. When she got there, he dropped his sign and scooped her up in a big hug. "Hillary! We finally meet. You're more beautiful than your photos." He pushed his sunglasses to the top of his head.

She was speechless for a moment. Michael was handsomer than his photo, but all the excitement and the travel was catching up to her. She felt slightly dizzy and realized she was holding her breath. She let it out slowly, as he released her. "Thank you," she said, her voice shaky.

"Let's go to baggage claim and make sure they treated your suitcases okay. Beautiful day here in London. I have so much to show you, but first I'm sure you need some rest. I've made all the arrangements at the hotel as you requested."

Hillary followed him toward Baggage claim. Although her father had offered to pay for everything, she'd insisted on only allowing him to pay the airfare and give her some travel money that had been converted into traveler's checks. When she'd written

Michael of her plans, he'd offered to book her into a good hotel that wasn't too expensive.

After gathering her suitcases that she'd tied a red ribbon to in order to identify easier, she and Michael left the airport through the underground parking area. Michael stopped in back of a blue Honda Civic, placed her bags by his side, reached in his slacks pocket and took out a key ring. "Give me your case," he said. "I'll put it in the boot with your luggage."

Michael's use of the English term for a car trunk made her realize she was actually in England. After her suitcases were loaded into the "boot" of his car and they were driving toward the hotel, she was reminded again when Michael drove on the left side of the road.

She couldn't help marvel at the loveliness of the city as she watched the buildings pass by. She caught a glimpse of Big Ben further away and caught her breath. Michael turned to her, but she couldn't read his eyes because he'd put on his sunglasses. "I'm so glad we could finally meet, my dear Hillary. Do you mind if I play the radio? I enjoy music while I drive, and there will be plenty of time for us to talk later."

"Of course," Hillary said, pleased that he had the manners to ask her permission. "I enjoy music, too." Even though her arrival in England and introduction to Michael had gone well, she was still nervous and hoped the music would relax her. She'd promised to call her father as soon as she'd checked into her room, and she planned to do that.

Michael turned the black knob on the car's console and adjusted it so that the music wasn't too loud. Words sung by a throaty female voice drifted through the speakers. It was a familiar song that was popular in the U.S., Anita Bakers' "Sweet Love." Michael rolled down the window, and the cool wind whipped her hair. "I love that song," she said.

Michael smiled. "So do I, and now it's even more special to me. I'll always remember it as our meeting song."

Hillary thought that was sweet. She was thinking of a reply when Michael pulled over in front of the St. George's Hotel. A doorman in a gold jacket stood outside the blue awning of the building. "They have valet service here," Michael said. He opened his door and then came around to let Hillary out. He'd left the car running with the keys in the ignition but opened the trunk (or, boot as he called it) with another set. A porter with a luggage trolley came by and took Hillary's cases and then a valet got behind the wheel. Michael guided Hillary toward the glass revolving doors that led into the hotel's checkout desk and lobby.

As they entered, Hillary was awestruck. The interior of the hotel was gleaming with burnished wood paneling and highly polished floors. "Let me take care of check in," Michael said. "You just have a seat and rest. I'll join you in a few minutes." He indicated some comfortable window seating that looked out upon the bustling buildings and shops of Regent Street.

Hillary sat on a gold cushioned circular chair and watched as Michael waited on the check-in line glancing back and smiling at her. She felt lucky to be traveling to a foreign place in the company of a friend she felt she'd known forever. Something inside her was blooming, and the excitement was bubbling forth.

When Michael appeared beside her, she woke from her reverie. He had two glasses in his hands. She hadn't even seen him go to the discrete bar across the way.

"We must toast to your first trip to London," he said sitting across from her. There were others in their vicinity, but she felt that she was alone with him. She took the champagne glass he handed her. "I'll toast to that." She raised her glass, already giddy. Michael gently clunked his glass against hers and drank the champagne down straight. She felt a bit embarrassed when she just sipped it, but he made no comment. "There's something I want to give you," he said instead. Reaching in his pocket, he withdrew a small dark jewelry box.

Hillary held her breath. Maybe she should've had more to drink.

"This has been passed down from my great grandmother to all the women in my family. I don't have a sister, so my mother gave it to me to pass to my wife." He saw the frightened look on her face and added, "For now, it's just a token of friendship to a special lady. Hillary, you have no idea how you've helped me through your letters.

I'm subject to depression, but you've brightened up my life. I tend to be shy, but through our letters, I was able to overcome that. I've shared with you so much of me that I feel we're closer than if we had grown up together."

Hillary looked into his eyes now unhidden behind the sunglasses he'd tucked in his shirt pocket. The warmth she saw there touched her heart. "I feel the same way, Michael."

"Open it." He handed her the box.

She carefully pulled back the black velvet top to reveal a diamond ring in a simple white gold setting. It wasn't extravagant by any means but because it was a family heirloom, she knew the value it represented. "Oh, Michael. You didn't have to give me anything."

"Please." He waved off her modesty. "You deserve it, sweet Hillary. Wear it for me."

She slid the ring onto the finger of her right hand because the left hand would be meant for an engagement ring, and as prone to romanticizing as she was, she wasn't ready to think of that yet.

"It looks lovely on you. Does it fit well?"

"Yes. Thank you so much, Michael, but I can't keep it."

"Hold off that decision until your trip is over," he said. "Meanwhile, we can go up to the room, so you can rest before dinner." He reached in his pocket again and took out two hotel card keys. "Our room is on the 9th floor. Are you ready to go?"

"Our room?" Hillary was surprised. She'd expected him to book separate rooms.

"I'm sorry," he said quickly. "There seems to have been an overbooking problem. I could only get one room for us, but don't worry. There's a couch in the room where I can sleep."

Hillary figured this was fine. She wouldn't tell her father about the situation, though. It would just make him worry. She was a grown woman now, and he'd trusted her to travel alone, so sharing a room with a close friend shouldn't be an issue. "Okay. Let's go then."

Michael smiled as he placed his empty champagne glass on the table in front of their seats where she'd left her half full one. "Very well. Tomorrow, your friend Clara will meet us here, and we can all travel together. Maybe you two would want to do some shopping while I take care of a few things. I've managed to have the week off from work, but my boss may want me to put in a few hours. After that, I have a full itinerary planned for us and a few surprises."

Hillary stood up. She felt slightly tipsy but knew it couldn't have been the few sips of wine she'd swallowed. Maybe it was the flight and the time zone change. She'd mentioned Clara to Michael and was happy that he didn't mind her coming along with them. She followed him to the bank of lifts and waited while he pressed the up button to take them to the 9th floor.

The room was halfway down the long hall on the right. Michael inserted the hotel card key and deftly pulled it out when the security light turned green. Pushing the door open, he switched on the light, and let Hillary step into the room ahead of him. Hillary was struck again by the opulence of the hotel. She told herself she had nothing to compare it to because she'd never traveled anywhere before, but it still seemed amazing. There was a king-sized bed with a golden bedspread that matched the polished wood of the bed frame, nightstand, and dresser. As Michael had promised, there was a couch and sitting area with table and chairs. A room to the side led to a bathroom with a marble sink and glass fixtures. The walls were a pale lemon and featured photos of London attractions – Big Ben, a red double-decker sightseeing bus, a sign at the Tube station. All the frames were gold, keeping with the royal theme of the room.

"I see red and gold are London's colors," she said.

"Indeed. Now, Miss Johnson. Please have a seat or wash up in the loo if you'd like. I know your stomach's probably on states' time, but don't worry, there's a fine restaurant downstairs in which we can dine tonight."

Hillary still couldn't get used to the foreign terms. Just as she was about to take a seat on the bed, there was a knock on the door. Michael opened it to the bellhop with their bags. He took some bills out of his pocket and handed it to the man on his way out, and the smile the man returned indicated that it was a nice tip.

"You can start unpacking if you'd like," Michael said. "I have to take care of a few things downstairs, but

I won't be too long. I'll be back to take you to dinner if you'd like to change, but the restaurant is casual, so wear whatever you would like."

Hillary laughed, although she was a bit uncomfortable with being left alone in a foreign hotel room. On the other hand, she was glad for time to herself to phone her father to let him know she'd arrived safely in England.

The rest of the evening went well. After Michael returned to the room, he escorted her to dinner. It seemed he'd been able to reserve a table for two in a corner away from the main part of the restaurant. The lights were low, and a candle cast a flickering glow across his face as he sat across from her. When she was confused about some of the items on the menu, he interpreted their American counterparts. The dessert, Yorkshire pudding, was a surprise. She'd expected a pudding, but it turned out to be more of a popover. She found it delicious. As they finished their meals, Michael said, "I have an itinerary planned for us tomorrow. You look tired from your travels, so we should call it a night soon."

"Aren't we meeting Clara?" she asked.

Michael lowered his eyes. "I'm sorry. I meant to tell you. She called the hotel and left a message for you. Something came up. She won't be able to join us after all."

Hillary wasn't duly disappointed, but she inquired,

"So is she free another day this week? I would like to meet her."

Michael shook his head slightly and then looked across at her. "I'm afraid she's tied up all week, but don't worry, you'll visit again and meet her. In the meantime," he grinned, "I think I'll make a nice tourist guide for you."

Despite her exhaustion, Hillary had a hard time falling to sleep in an unfamiliar bed. She was also nervous about Michael being in the outer room and felt bad that he had to sleep on the couch. She offered to switch with him every other night, but he insisted that she was his guest and that he was such a sound sleeper that nothing bothered him. She felt lucky that he was such a gentleman and looked forward to visiting with him on all the tour stops that he had in mind.

The next day was another bright and sunny one as they left the hotel after breakfast. Michael had donned his sunglasses again and opened the passenger side of his car to help her get in. "Since it's such a nice day, I thought we'd visit St. James's Park," he announced as he started the engine. Then I'd like to take you to a special place." She wondered what he had in mind.

The Park was huge and beautiful. She'd been to several parks where she lived, but they paled in comparison to this one. As they walked together,

Michael offered her his hand. She took it, and they strolled through the park. Michael was a perfect tour guide and gave her a quick overview of the park. "St. James's Park is one of London's eight royal parks," he explained. "It includes the Mall, a processional route in honor of Queen Victoria, which has seen innumerable historic Royal processions including coronations, state openings of Parliament and state visits. The Park is also surrounded by landmarks such as Buckingham Palace, Clarence House, and Whitehall. If we have time, we can visit them today or another day before you leave, but I want to get you to the other place I mentioned."

Hillary was enthralled as they passed fountains, statues, and a lake. When they came across a group of pelicans, she exclaimed in delight.

"Those birds have lived in St James's Park for nearly 400 years. They were originally presented as a gift from the Russian Ambassador to King Charles II," Michael told her.

Hillary had brought a camera with her to take photos of the sights, but she was afraid she'd use up her film's camera roll on the first day of her trip, so she tried her best to limit the number she took.

When their tour of the park ended, she was slightly disappointed because she could've spent the whole day in that beautiful place, but she was also eager to see the surprise Michael had promised her for that afternoon.

"Where are we going?" she asked as they drove

along the highway which became more rural as they headed west.

Michael glanced at her through his sunglasses. "We're going to Wales. The surprise I have for you is located there."

"Wales? We're leaving England?"

He grinned. "It's not too far. Sit back. Relax. We should be there in a few hours."

"A few hours?" It was already 1 p.m. Hillary didn't like the idea of returning in the dark, but Michael read her thoughts. "Don't worry. We'll be back before nightfall."

The long drive was worth it. Hillary began to relax as they started passing farms and saw sheep and cows grazing. Used to living in a city, she was happy for the opportunity to view the countryside outside of London.

When they finally arrived at their destination, pulling up at a castle, Hillary was indeed surprised.

"I bet you've never been to a real castle," Michael said, removing his sunglasses and smiling at her. "This is Chepstow Castle. It was built in 1067, a year after William the Conqueror became king." He related more history to her, but she didn't hear much of it because she was gazing in awe at the structure situated on a cliff over a river that Michael said was the River Wye.

"You look awestruck," he pointed out. "Come. I'll show you around."

After Michael parked his car, they made their way up the gravel path toward the castle. Hillary noted that no one else seemed to be around. She was thankful for the privacy, but slightly nervous about being in such an isolated place she didn't know.

"There are some places you can climb up for a view," Michael said. "I'll help you." It seemed he was quite familiar with the castle and led her to a ledge with a foothold. She followed him, mounting the narrow steps into the castle. He gave her a hand up at the last step and they stood in an opening gazing across at the magnificent view. She felt her heart race, but knew it wasn't just from the climb. Suddenly, Michael leaned over and gave her a light kiss on the lips, smiling as he did so. She felt as if she were in a fairytale in a castle and that it was all part of a love story in which she played the main part and Michael was her knight in shining armor.

The spell was broken when Michael suggested they tour the rest of the castle. They spent an hour or so walking around and then some other tourists started showing up, by which time they decided to leave.

"Did you enjoy that?" Michael asked as they were heading back to London.

While Hillary knew he was talking about the castle, she couldn't help but blush. "Very much so. Thank you."

"Tomorrow, we'll visit some friends of mine. They live outside London."

"Do your parents live nearby?" She was curious

about Michael's family. While she'd told him about her dad, he hadn't spoken about any of his relatives.

"My parents are abroad right now. My father's in the Royal Air Force, and they travel a lot. I've been on my own since finishing Sixth Form." When she gave him a puzzled look, he explained that sixth form was the term for college. She already knew, from his letters, that he was an only child like her.

"Do you live nearby?" She recalled the postmark on his letters but wasn't familiar with the London addresses.

He shook his head. "No. I have a flat on the other side of the city, but it's not much to see. I'd much rather show you my office at the British Library, which is one of the places on our itinerary for the rest of the week."

They arrived back at the hotel in time for a late dinner. The next day, they took a short drive to the countryside beyond London and visited two couples, friends of Michael's, who were renting a house for the summer. When he introduced her to them, he referred to her as his "friend from the States" which she realized irked her somewhat because she was hoping he would call her his girlfriend. She also felt left out, despite their friendliness, when they shared private jokes and talked about events she hadn't been part of. One of the two women, Emma, kept eyeing her as if measuring her for something, which made her even more uncomfortable. She was relieved when they finally left.

Hillary found the rest of the week more pleasant. She

enjoyed her visit to the British Library and found Michael's co-workers both knowledgeable and witty. On the last night of the trip, they had a pleasant dinner in the hotel's restaurant.

"I can't believe I'm leaving tomorrow," she said. "The week went so fast. Thank you so much for being an excellent guide."

He smiled. "You were an excellent guest. Let's toast to our continued friendship and much more." He raised the glass of wine he'd poured from the bottle that had been brought to the table.

She took a sip of the wine. "I hope we do keep in touch, Michael. I'd love to visit here again and meet your family when they're at home."

"Of course, you will. I'll give you my phone number. Call any time. I'd also like to keep writing to you." He gazed into her eyes and reached over to touch her hand, rubbing the ring he'd given her as a gift. "One day, this will have a special meaning to both of us."

Hillary's heart fluttered at his words, but they were the last thing she remembered. Even though she'd only taken a sip of the wine and hadn't been unduly tired, she must've fallen asleep because she woke up hours later in her hotel bed. As her eyes adjusted to the light, she realized she wasn't alone. Michael lay next to her. She had no recollection of inviting him there or even walking to the room. A terrible thought ran through her mind. Despite being quite sheltered, she knew about roofies, drugs that men slipped into their dates' drinks to render them unconscious. Had Michael done that to her? She started to become suspicious as questions built up in her head –the way his friend Emma had stared at her, the fact he hadn't introduced her to his parents, and why Clara had never joined them.

Panicking, she was about to get out of bed, pack her bags quickly, and leave the hotel even though her flight wasn't leaving that soon. Right then, Michael woke up and, still groggy, said, "Hey, there. Did you sleep well? You were out like a light last night. I brought you up to the room. Not to criticize your weight or anything, but after carrying you, I pulled my back and couldn't imagine sleeping on the couch. I hope you don't mind." When he noticed her expression, he smiled slightly and added, "No worries. I slept way in the corner. See, I still have my clothes on."

Although that still didn't convince Hillary, she tried to accept the explanation. Her clothes, as well, were on, and other than her anxiety, she felt fine.

At the airport, they said goodbye. He kissed her very properly on the cheeks and then lightly on the lips. "I'll write soon," he whispered, tracing her right ring finger once more, "and call every day."

The long journey home had her musing on her time in England – the lovely St. James' Park, the fairytale-like Chepstow Castle in Wales, the shops along Regents Street, the funny terms for car trunks, elevators, and certain foods. It all came back in a rush, but so did the doubt about the course of the previous night. Despite her uncertainty about Michael's intentions, she didn't regret her adventure, and when she landed in a horrible rainstorm at JFK airport with her father meeting her with a large red umbrella, she pasted a smile on her face and told him she'd had a wonderful time.

The next few days after the trip, she cycled between sleeping off the extreme jet lag and checking her messages as soon as she woke, desperate to hear from Michael. She jumped every time the phone rang hoping it was him, proving her concerns about him were wrong. But he never called. He also never wrote. When her jet lag was finally over, depression set in. She read over his letters incessantly. Were they all lies? She spent a lot of time in her room and, when her father asked what was wrong, she said she was still tired from the trip. She found it interesting that he never asked about Michael or what she'd seen or done in England, although she'd shared some of the happier stories. She had a feeling that he knew things hadn't gone the way she'd hoped. She wondered if he'd noticed the ring on her finger that she still refused to take off.

After a month, Hillary tried to snap out of her malaise. She called Michael, but the phone number he gave said the line was disconnected. With tears in her eyes, she wrote him a letter asking for some explanations and enclosed the ring he'd given her. She never received a reply. She also wrote to Clara but never got an answer from her either.

While her memories were tainted by what happened

between her and Michael, Hillary felt as though she'd grown through the experience and tried to focus on the better parts of her trip, recalling the majestic view from the castle and the sunlit flowers of the park. Her travels to England and newly gained experiences coaxed her out of her previously shy, closed-off self, and she realized she could just as well make friends in person rather than relying on letters.

The Great London Eye

N M Haider

The great London Eye
In a wonderful
Time capsule I fly by
Roaming London's blue and grey skies
Drones compete for airpace
Like the London eye
Oh how lucky am I?
I peer down below
London city in its glory
Is for show
Slavery ghosts ships
Silently still row
Human cargo and values
Overboard they throw
The drone engineers
Our thoughts they know
Buckingham palace
Gardens perfectly mowed
Their scandals we know
Spanish pirates who swam
To queen Eliz's bed
Hyde Park runners
Puff as they trot and tread
Pride festivals in the park
Robots and humans wed
We were humans once
In London once they said
A new era for the city
Robots speak and reign and are witty
Hovercrafts and robots fly by
To myself a passenger
To history and the future
Of the great London eye

London Bridge's Prophecy

Katrenia G. Busch

London bridge
Is here to stay
Strong and steady it shall be
London bridge
Is here to stay
Sang the lady borne of the sea

London bridge
Shall reign and be
Vikings heard the prophecy
London bridge
Shall reign and be
Spoken again by Aphrodite

London bridge
Is here to stay
Strong and steady it shall be
London bridge
Is here to stay
Sang she borne of gay-la-lee

"WILL KEMP'S TURN - A MONOLOGUE

REX MCGREGOR

A former comedian meets the rival who replaced him.

Character: WILL KEMP, a retired actor, 40s to 60s

Setting: Hampstead Heath, London

Time: 1602

Will enters, shabbily dressed.

WILL

Is this a blasted heath I see before me?

With no applauding audience to adore me.

The desolation singularly apt

For one on whose poor head cruel Fortune's crapped.

Must I soliloquize in solitude?
No. Someone doth approach. A chance for food.
Perchance 'tis some kind soul who'll give a groat,
If not a ruffian who'll slit my throat.
All's one. A crust will bring my belly peace.
Or else a dagger grants a swift release.

Good morrow, friend, if I may be so bold.
Canst spare a coin or two? "Poor Tom's acold."
Fie! Dost thou walk away e'en while I beg?
Thou currish motley-minded pigeon-egg!

I see thou turnest round and comest back.
Not looking generous, alack, alack.
But hold. I recognize that scowling frown.
You're Robert Armin, London's latest clown.
I saw you in *Twelfth Night*. You played the jester.
What was the fellow's name? Ooze-Pus? Or Fester?
My little joke. I'm also in the trade.
Or was, till I was cast into the shade.
'Tis I. Will Kemp. You must remember me.
You took my place in Shakespeare's company.
Oft-times, my Falstaff made the groundlings roar.
My Dogberry had them clamoring for more.
My star shone brightly then. Thine was the lesser.
Now, thou outshinest thy poor predecessor.

Our William loathed my keen extemporizing.
That spelled the end of me and my revising.
Inserted jokes offend his precious taste.
My merry japes are banished. What a waste!
Will rules the roost and nothing undermines
The boring parroting of boring lines.
You sing, "The rain, it raineth every day."
You call that wit? A weather forecast? Nay!
The public hardly wait with bated breath
For your depressing "Come 'way, come 'way, Death!"
Once, jolly jigs and fun were all the rage.
Now, fool-philosophers infest the stage.

Who needs your coins? I live on mockery.
Deriding you is food and drink to me.

THE GHOSTS YOU BRING HOME

MATT MCGEE

I'd always wanted my own library. Not a sprawling repository of musty-smelling books with loose pages that look better on shelves than they do when you try to read them. What I wanted was a home for the greatest contemporary volumes. *The Girl on the Train* and *Perks of Being a Wallflower* and *Me & Kev* for starters. Everything would be alphabetical. Only hardbound editions would do. With help from the internet, I could track them all down.

I'd always imagined this library would be laid out the way I'd imagined Jack Benny's might've been on the old radio shows I've heard. "*I need to speak to you in private, Jackson,*" Phil Harris would say, and Jack would reply, "Alright, Phil. Let's go into the library," or "Let's step into my study." And there, business would get handled.

And like Benny's study, the books wouldn't be the

only attraction. It would be the stories behind their acquisition, a life's knowledge gathered from different continents, smaller cities and towns so worn they might blow away any moment.

I haven't spent a lot of money on books. But I have spent a considerable amount on travel that's led me *to* books. Like the English language bookstore in Madrid (*Meshugah* by IB Singer) and Shakespeare & Co. in Paris (*Best American Short Stories of 1998* – how did that get there?). When a book has a story behind its acquisition, it makes it that much more valuable to the collection.

And no book has brought more mystery than the one on an eye-level shelf in my new study, the small blood-red volume I stumbled across ten years ago in a small London thrift store.

By the time I traveled to England, most everyone I knew had read *Hound of the Baskervilles,* one of the scariest tales ever told. Without it we'd have never had *An American Werewolf in London,* a landmark in trans-Atlantic cinema if ever there was one. And once they're seen, no one can forget the gory scenes on the moor where the American hikers get theirs.

I first saw the movie as a kid on a freshly-minted VHS tape. Afterward, I promised myself two things: one, I'd never hitchhike through England, and two, I'd stay far, far away from moors, whatever they were.

I managed to stay out of England for the first forty years of my life but then the bug bit, at an age when I'd made enough friends around the globe to justify a tour. One of these pals was Syd, whose family just happened to be in possession of a hotel off Kensington High Street. I'd simply hoped that my former band mate would just make sure I didn't sleep on the street.

When I called and told him I was coming, he said in his best Keith Richards drawl, "Just get on a plane, mate! Just get over here!" He said it like it was no big deal. Hop in your car and drive over.

It really was that easy. I booked a flight, threw a copy of Brian Gruley's latest Michigan mystery into a bag on top of a few days' clothes, drove to LAX and, eleven hours later, was riding the underground leaving Heathrow.

Wasn't Syd surprised.

"HEY!"

I dropped my bag in front of the desk and in typical Keith Richards-esque fashion he wasn't going to let any old registration portal obstruct a reunion. He leapt feet first, and like a long-lost lover I caught all hundred ten pounds of him. An on-off heroin habit does that to a body. He weighed considerably less than some of my actual long-lost lovers.

Twenty minutes later, with pints in our hands, he leaned an elbow on the bar of the Goat Tavern. Chelsea was playing Man U. so the place was a madhouse.

"So what are you doing on this side of the pond?" he shouted.

I sipped brown foam onto my upper lip then licked it away. The stuff really does taste better over there.

"Just needed a chance to get away and read in peace."

"Don't you have quiet little bookstores in your country?"

"Bookstores, yes. Small? No."

"You know what I've been wanting to read lately is I hear Keith's got a new book out. It's called *Life*. Heard of it?"

"I was in the Strand in New York when they were unpacking it. Maybe we could walk down to a bookstore later and pick up a copy or two."

"Deal. So which library did you come all this way to hide out in?"

"Don't know. Which one do you recommend?"

He smirked his best Keith Richards-esque smirk and tugged on a coat that might have come from the Queen's donation bin.

"C'mon now, do I look like the library type?"

His hair seemed permanently teased. Everything, from his boney cheekbones to the sunken eyes, his rail-thin figure to the veins bulging from his arms said *I'm a rock star, and my kind are fading from the Earth.*

"Well," he started, "I don't know much about books, but I can tell you this – you're gonna need a coat no matter how long you decide to stay."

I looked down at the hockey jersey I'd worn. "Not enough?"

"What is that thing you've got on, anyway? Hopefully it's warm, because I might as well tell you now, there's no heat in your room."

Maybe he saw the panic on my face.

I found out through trial and error, the error having just showed up at Syd's hotel without consulting even a *Fodor Travel Guide*, that I wouldn't just need a good coat. I needed Dick Van Dyke to come sweep the chimney of the fireplace in the old room, along with a cord of wood to keep warm.

Syd was right. The radiator was useless. Its main valve had rusted shut, who knew why or how long ago. The windows needed caulking; cold air seemed to come straight across the channel from France just to whistle around the glass. The faucet had worn a spot in the porcelain sink with its endless dripping. The shower could use a once-over as well; I found after a mostly sleepless night that most of its pressure sprayed out the sides.

On my first morning in London, I made a list and hopped aboard a genuine double-decker bus. Six blocks away was a hardware store, and I arrived with old parts in hand. The odds and ends I needed cost less than three Pounds and a couple disposable tools only two Pounds more. By mid-afternoon I had a quiet faucet, the long-dead radiator was delivering steam heat once again, and a sealed window faced out onto Kensington Park. Lucky for this traveling Yank, the hardware store employed an old English man who knew where to dig up proper old English parts.

I was standing in the shower, clearing the rust and scale from the inside of the nozzle, settling its new sealing washer in place when Syd knocked on the door.

"Neighbor says she's hearing a lot of banging in here. Wanted to make sure you didn't have a broad in your room. And if you did, why didn't you call me up at the desk and send for help? So, what's all this."

I pointed out the newly sealed window. Set my palm on a working radiator. Showed off the quiet faucet. "Shower's almost done. All it needed was this washer and a spot of sealer."

"Good golly Miss Molly. You didn't have to do all this."

"Already done."

"You're on vacation."

I shrugged. "Guy who knows how to fix things never really goes on vacation. I once had a rental car, blew a heater hose in a crappy neighborhood outside San Francisco. Pulled up to a closed service station, took out a knife, cut six inches off their garden hose and limped back to Atascadero."

"*Atascadero.* Sounds like a place for bullfighting."

"In the morning I bought some real hose and drove

back to LA. But not until I stopped by this leftist bookstore and found a great read on the evils of capitalism."

"You and your books. Look, still, you didn't have to do all this, mate. I got a man does these things."

Syd must have been able to read my face.

"OK, alright," he conceded. "Maybe he's not really on the job, but. Hey... you wanna job?"

"I couldn't stay. Even with you vouching as my employer, the best I can do is a six month work Visa. Then the coppers come knocking for me."

I set the cheap channel locks down. The nozzle was back in place, a dab of sealer on its threads. "Stand back."

I turned the knobs. Water blasted out of the showerhead. "Compared to the dribble I rinsed off in this morning that's a geyser."

"Well done mate."

I shut it off. "Better than new."

He looked around and in his best Keith Richards drawl said "Well then! From here on out this will be known as the Bridal Suite. Nicest room in the place now, it is."

"I'll just be glad to have a quiet, warm place to sleep and a shower that works in the morning."

"How much I owe you?"

I put the channel lock pliers into his hand. "Give these to your man Friday. As for what you owe me, you can do me one thing..."

"What's that."

"Put on that old coat of yours and walk me to the nearest used bookstore."

Syd and I went to a local shop selling new books. We each bought a copy of *Life*. That night, I met his sister who, it turns out, is pretty handy with computers. Not 'hacking government websites' kind of handy, but the following morning, after my long and deliberately hot shower, I found Syd in the lobby, holding a slip of paper.

"So. You start with Oxfam around the corner…"

"What's Oxfam?"

"It's like you Yanks and your Goodwill. Like the Salvation Army."

"Perfect. Secondhand store."

"Precisely. So you start with them bleedin' hearts, then there's a whole list of places that Prissy worked up here."

I took the paper and nodded my thanks.

"And if you're feelin' real adventurous," he pointed, "there's Shakespeare and Company."

"Where's that?"

"Paris. You take the tube, go to Kings Cross station, and there's the Eurorail. It takes you thru the Chunnel to Paris."

I nodded. "Tomorrow."

"Better idea, mate. Give Paris a whole day anyway. At least. Meet a cute French girl. Bring one home for me. You know what they say. France's greatest exports are sex and art."

"You keep saying all this like you can't get girls on your own."

He puffed out the side of his face, the way aging rock stars are apt to do. "Shoot. I can get 'em, keepin' 'em's my problem. You on the other hand.."

"I spend all my time haunting bookstores."

"Yeah, them places are fulla cute girls. Smart women. Just your type. Tell ya what, offer 'em to fix up their plumbing like you did ours and you'll be the belle of the ball."

"I'm too busy browsing shelves."

"Maybe I *should* go with you. Make sure you get into trouble instead of just reading about the people who've done it. Yeah. I should go haunt up a few bookstores, I think."

Haunting was something Syd knew. Shop owners loved seeing his semi-famous face in their establishments; he rarely had to pay for anything. But lately, the listeners whose tastes had 'evolved' past his style of songwriting rarely looked his way, like it were bad luck to look a ghost in the eye.

"Yeah," I finally said. "Why don't you come haunt this Oxfam with me?"

"Nah, I gotta go cook up lunch."

I knew better than to interrupt. Syd's cooking only required a lighter and a spoon.

"Besides," he said, "buying Keith's book yesterday satisfied my reading pleasure for the next decade. For you though it's something else. That library in your head is pretty much where you live."

I looked around at the hotel lobby on the other side of the world. A street full of handsome cabs and pedestrians with classy accents passed by.

"I don't know. Lately I've been feeling more like a citizen of the world."

"Good. Now go bring some of that home."

I walked Kensington High Street, beneath the shadow of history, thinking about what Syd had said. I took out the slip of paper and followed his sister's directions. I walked faster, expecting a mammoth, factory-sized operation like back home. Blue-vested workers would process thousands of daily donations, tending racks of clothing, and rows of appliances, toys and books.

What I found in Kensington's high-rent district was a boutique. The Oxfam shop looked so painfully stereotypical, so *English*, it was all I could do to stand on the sidewalk and take it in. Evening was falling, the streetlights were blinking as they woke up for work, glowing against the frontage of the little shop. It had narrow, wood-framed glass pane windows, and two limestone steps led to its door. I wondered how anything could fit into the place. Shoppers would bump elbows. Not something we did in California. Personal body space is a big deal.

"Allo."

The lady behind the counter, with a register that definitely looked like a pre-war antique itself, smiled a stained grin and set one hand against the countertop.

"Can I 'elp you find something?"

I smiled. I'd grown up on *Benny Hill* reruns.

"Books?"

She lifted her non-leaning arm, draped in burgundy cable-knit. "Right over there, you'll find a few books. Let us know if you need a hand."

I thanked her and moved to the shelf.

Twelve books. I'd crossed the Atlantic for a dozen library and grade school discards. Keith's 400-page volume was starting to look pretty good, as was a train ride to Paris.

Then, I saw it.

The squat red hardbound volume wore six lifetimes of bumps and scrapes. Black lettering on its spine announced this was an English printed and bound copy of *The Hound of the Baskervilles*. OK I thought, buying this English story in a London bookshop, clever enough. Only three pounds. What the hell. I brought it to the sweater lady.

"Find something, did we?"

"Yeah."

"Ah, good old Sherlock. Always a good read. Though I have to admit I don't fancy your American version of him, what with Robert Downey jr running around, snorting things up his nose, shooting up his veins, brawling in pits and whatnot."

I thought of the hotel where I'd left my few worldly belongings.

"Sherlock," she said, "he always beat everyone with his brains. Now you Yanks think he should be beating everyone's brains out, eh?"

She put the small receipt inside the cover as a bookmark and I turned away.

"I don't work in the movie industry," I said.

"Oh I didn't mean you!" she reached without touching, maybe sensing I was from LA. "It's just that this latest interpretation isn't to my liking, that's all."

I held up the small book. "Guess I'll just stick with the classics in their classic form."

"Good boy. Best way that. You never know what you'll find in a book, especially an old one."

I nodded slowly and closed the door. With the small volume under my arm like the schoolboy I'll never stop being, I took the cue of the sun setting over Kensington Palace and walked back to Syd's, one more piece of the library fallen into place.

"Whatcha' got there?"

I was in a big poofy chair, legs crossed at the knees. I held the red volume out for Syd to read the title on the spine.

"*Hound of the Baskervilles*."

"Found it in the Oxfam store."

Syd went to the window to air out the room. The fresh calking stopped him. I watched him tug a few more times until he figured it out.

"How can you stand it in here? It's like a bloody sauna."

"I'm from LA, we like things a little warm. Not too warm. Just right."

"Bunch of wankers." Syd sat on a chair that looked like it had been reupholstered in the 1960's. "How can you go on vacation and read all day?"

"It's raining out there."

"It's London!"

I was about to say *it can rain all it wants without me walking around in it*, but then I turned the page. And there on the left side were the three lines that would change the whole trip–and set the standard for every used book I'd ever buy.

Syd was still talking while I sat frozen, processing what I was seeing. A red stamp on the book's inside cover declared it had been discarded in 1969. It had belonged to a small school for boys during its prime, then stored after that, its pages unread ever since. Now I read the hand-written lines over and over:

FOR THOSE ABOUT TO ROCK
WE SALUTE YOU
WE SALUTE YOU

It was hand-written in pencil by someone not yet sure of their alphabet. Slowly, reeling with surprise, I said:

"Syd...?"

"Yeah."

"When did AC/DC's 'For Those About to Rock' come out?"

He pfft'ed. "What do I look like, some rock music historian?"

"Yes."

"Fair enough. 'Those About to Rock?' I'd say about... 1982? Somewhere in there?"

I held up the book where he could see. "Then explain this."

Syd took the book. He squinted. "I 'aven't got me glasses." He held the book at full arm's length. He read the familiar lyrics, scrawled into Page 54.

For those about to rock
We salute you
We salute you

He tilted the book again. "So?"

"That book was discarded in 1969. Stored in a box somewhere until the school donated it to Oxfam."

"So?"

"So! That song didn't come out for another decade. Jesus Christ, I think I've got Angus Young's schoolbook."

"Well I suppose that's interesting."

"Interesting?!"

"In some mild curiosity kind of way."

"Mild -" I stopped. "That's not mild curiosity. You're holding a piece of rock and roll history!"

He tossed the book back to me.

"So? I hold a piece of rock and roll history every time I take a pee. Why is this interesting to me?"

"Angus Young's schoolbook. I'm now the owner of the earliest known hand-written copy of 'Those About to Rock's' lyrics. This is a treasure."

"It's a discarded copy of *Hound of the Baskervilles* mate. For all you know some bored school kid scribbled that down."

"Not if the book had been taken out of circulation years before the song was written."

"Well," Syd said, got out of his chair and picked up the house phone. The hotel was old enough to still have them. "There's only one way to settle this."

Syd pulled out a little black book. I looked over his shoulder. He had Steven Tyler's cell number. Courtney Love's house phone. He flipped a couple pages. He dialed the number.

"Angus! Hey baby, how's rock and roll? Still lots of songs in those magic fingers?" Pause. "New ones? Awright."

"Well look Angus, I know this is going to seem like the oddest question you ever heard but I gotta ask. Kinda on behalf of a shy friend of mine who spends too much time reading."

Pause. "No, he's not media. Fuck me. It's something else."

"Yeah. OK, here it is. You ever read *Hound of the Baskervilles*?"

Syd listened.

"Yeah. Yeah, that one."

Pause.

"Yeah. Any chance this was while you was in school? Uh-huh. Yeah. OK. Yeah, I will. I said I will! I'll do it right now! Give my best to the band and let me hear those songs rather than later you slag. Alright, take care. Love you man."

Syd hung up. My eyes were bulging.

"So?"

Syd lit a cigarette. "He wants his book back."

"*What?*"

"He said yeah he's read it. Way back in school days. And if some wanker stumbles across his old copy then make sure he gets it back."

"This from the man who made millions dressing up like an English schoolboy and strutting around for forty years."

"And playing the fuck out of a guitar, don't forget. Shit, I forgot to get his address!"

Syd picked up the phone. Then he set it down again. He plopped back into the big poofy chair, the kind you can disappear in and read a classic English novel.

"Ah, fuck it. I'll call him again next year."

"By then I'll be back in America."

"With Angus's book safely on one of your shelves no doubt."

"He isn't going to show up at my house, is he?"

"Would be hard to explain to the neighbors, wouldn't it? Grown man dressed like a schoolboy, banging on your door in the middle of the night. Nah. He's got other fish to fry. Just put it in your will. Donate it to one of them Rock and Roll Cafés or whatever you Yanks've got out there."

"Hard Rock Café."

"Yeah, that. Good golly Miss Molly, I hope my chonies don't wind up in one of them places."

"*Chonies*? You really did bring some things back from LA, didn't you."

"I must have 'cause here you are."

"The Yankee flu. Coming back around." There was a quiet moment. "I promise not to do it again."

"What."

"Come back here."

"Nah. Come back often as you like." Syd leaned forward and stood. "That reminds me. Gig tonight. Come along."

"For what, to carry your guitar?"

"Yeah. No, bring that book a' yours."

"And what, read aloud to people?"

"Yeah, no. It's a storytellers thing. People wanna hear about my old days. You'll balance it out. Tell 'em what happened today."

I rode across London that night, thinking how I'll still be able to say I never went near a moor, or hiked into England much farther than to get myself to a soccer match near Shepard's Bush.

With Syd talking in the front passenger side, I bounced along in the non-existent backseat of his friend's Ford Fiesta, which is a whole different car in the UK, to a place called the Cock Tavern. Subtle. The host made me Syd's surprise warm-up act. From the stage I watched him mill about, smoke some pot, and drink whatever someone was buying.

The Angus Young story was a hit. In fact, it's been a hit everywhere I've gone. For three years I carried that blood red volume around the United States, telling the story on small stages. One host in Cincinnati played *Have a Drink on Me* as I took the stage. And more than a few people have offered far, far more than the original three pounds. My response has always been a polite *no*. Some things you have to find on your own.

Maybe the book will wind up in a Hard Rock Café, right next to a pair of Syd's chonies. Maybe it'll be sold off as part of my estate. Or maybe, some dark night, the creeping, arthritic fingers of an Australian rock star will sneak into my house, wanting to reclaim a piece of rock and roll history he never knew had been discarded, cast upon the waters to feed the book nerds of the world.

"RESTORING ROMEO" - A COMEDY

REX MCGREGOR

SYNOPSIS

Celebrated actor Charlotte Cushman wants to play Romeo, using Shakespeare's original text. But most of the cast protest. They demand the cleaned-up Garrick version.

CHARACTERS

Female

CHARLOTTE CUSHMAN, American actor, 29

SALLIE MERCER, Black American, Charlotte's dresser, 16

Male

EDWIN FORREST, American actor, 39

BENJAMIN (BEN) WEBSTER, English theatre manager, 48

PLACE

A dressing room in the Haymarket Theatre, London

TIME

December, 1845

Charlotte, dressed as Romeo, is struggling to write a letter. Sallie enters.

CHARLOTTE

Sallie.

SALLIE

Yes, Miss Charlotte.

CHARLOTTE

I'm writing to Rose. I fear my tone may be a trifle cold. Let me hear your opinion.

SALLIE

Do you desire a brutally honest critique?

CHARLOTTE

I'd like you to lend an impartial ear, but a sympathetic voice.

SALLIE

It's good to have clear instructions. Begin.

CHARLOTTE

"My dearest wife."

SALLIE

Modify the superlative.

CHARLOTTE

Too mawkish?

SALLIE

If you call her your *dearest* wife, she'll suspect you have others.

CHARLOTTE

"My darling wife. My tour of the provinces was a

dazzling success. I am back in London, shortly to commence an engagement at the Haymarket."

CHARACTER
SALLIE

Say "the prestigious Haymarket Theatre." Or she'll think it's a barn.

CHARLOTTE

You're such a snob, Sallie. I'll keep plain "Haymarket." "I have enjoyed playing Rosalind and Portia—women aping men. Now, I shall triumph as a genuine male character. Romeo. Opposite Susan as Juliet."

SALLIE

Put "my sister Susan." So Miss Rose won't get jealous. As well she might.

CHARLOTTE

I'm discreet in my amours.

SALLIE

She can read the change in your letters. A year ago, you were writing, "I miss your lips!"

CHARLOTTE

I miss missing her lips.

SALLIE

A sad decline, Miss Charlotte.

CHARLOTTE

One day, you'll learn. No heart is so small that it can embrace only one lover.

SALLIE

Not to mention all the deceit and betrayals and broken vows.

CHARLOTTE

No one should ever pledge their troth. We mistake passion for durability. And the particular for unique.

SALLIE

Have you written that?

CHARLOTTE

If only I could. There'd be much less unhappiness in the world if we were all authentic.

SALLIE

Authentic?

CHARLOTTE

True to our nature. I long for a colony of artists, where women can live openly and free.

SALLIE

In Boston? Or Philadelphia?

CHARLOTTE

Obviously, it will have to be someplace abroad.

Edwin enters, dressed as Tybalt.

EDWIN

Miss Cushman. Like unto an angel herald,
I trumpet forth the universe imperiled.

CHARLOTTE

Fie, Mr. Forrest. You forgot to knock.

EDWIN

So steeped in sin, you'll soon survive the shock.
Provoke a gentleman and he'll presume
To burst into a lady's dressing room.

CHARLOTTE

What? Have my charms enflamed you?

EDWIN

Do not jest.
I come here at the company's behest.

CHARLOTTE

Your constant rhyming, sir, is quite outrageous.

EDWIN

'Tis force of habit.

CHARLOTTE

And, I fear, contagious.

EDWIN

We worship Shakespeare. We repudiate
These changes you have introduced of late.
You dare replace the words on which we dote—

CHARLOTTE

With ones the writer actually wrote.

EDWIN

You tarnish his resplendent memory
By digging up a crude vulgarity
Which, in our cultured age, would scandalize.

CHARLOTTE

Your primness grants no right to vandalize.

EDWIN

It's you who are the vandal. How barbaric,
Deleting the improvements made by Garrick.

CHARLOTTE

I like a text that doesn't mollycoddle
The audience with sentimental twaddle.

EDWIN

Enough! The cast have delegated me
To issue unto you a stern decree.
Use Garrick's version. Or we shan't perform.

CHARLOTTE

They can't all be against me.

EDWIN

The whole swarm.

CHARLOTTE

My sister is a Shakespeare connoisseur.

EDWIN

I didn't even bother asking *her*.

SALLIE

Or me.

EDWIN

A dresser?

SALLIE

I play Balthasar
And the apothec'ry.

EDWIN

A budding star.
If we withdraw our labor, fill our shoes.
Play all the Capulets and Montagues.

CHARLOTTE

Hush, sir.

SALLIE

Wait! This will thwart his foul designs.
As prompter, I know everybody's lines.

CHARLOTTE

No need for that. Fetch Mr. Webster.

EDWIN

Yes.
Let's call on Ben to solve this blasted mess.

CHARLOTTE

As an enlightened impresario—

EDWIN

He knows, without a cast he has no show.

CHARLOTTE

A theatre manager yet has a soul.

EDWIN

Not Ben.

SALLIE

Miss C. Let me play every role.

CHARLOTTE

Fetch Mr. Webster, Sallie.

SALLIE

But—

CHARLOTTE

Be gone!

SALLIE

As thou command'st. I shall return anon.

Sallie exits.

CHARLOTTE

Now, sir. Reveal the motive for your malice.

EDWIN

Pray tell me. What do you suspect?

CHARLOTTE

You're jealous.
While my celebrity takes flight and soars,
The British public are ignoring yours.

EDWIN

This vile injustice makes me boil with rage.
The eminent tragedian of the age,
Reduced to playing Tybalt. Two short scenes!

CHARLOTTE

"Blink and you'll miss how Edwin Forrest preens."

EDWIN

I'll be the laughingstock of London town.

CHARLOTTE

That's why you're shutting this production down.
You aren't protecting Garrick's script at all.
You won't perform because your part's too small.

EDWIN

Thou hast impugned my honor. Draw thy sword!

CHARLOTTE

Base villain! Thou shalt reap thy just reward.
The great Macready taught me how to duel.

EDWIN

My rival feeds my fiery fury fuel.

Charlotte and Edwin have a dramatic sword fight.

Ben and Sallie enter.

BEN

Good. They're rehearsing now. Act Three,
Scene One.

SALLIE

The fight is real.

BEN

It's realistic fun.

CHARLOTTE

Hold! Ben, will you determine our dispute?

BEN

I'm sorry, Charlotte. I endorse his suit.
The public crave familiarity.
We'll stick with Garrick.

CHARLOTTE

Then you won't have me.

BEN

My dear, 'twill break my heart to see you leave.

EDWIN

The play must go on. There's no time to grieve.

CHARLOTTE

I thought your mission was to stop the show.

EDWIN

Since you're resigning, I'll play Romeo.

CHARLOTTE

I should have known the treachery of men.
I'll foil your crafty plan. — I'm staying, Ben.

BEN

You'll go with Garrick's version?

CHARLOTTE

I agree.

SALLIE

Miss Charlotte! What of authenticity?

CHARLOTTE

For current taste, the Bard's too rude and rough.
The Garrick changes don't go far enough.

BEN

There is an even cleaner text by Kemble.

CHARLOTTE

It keeps a flaw which makes a lady tremble.
The double suicide.

EDWIN

That drives the plot.
It's utterly essential.

CHARLOTTE

No, it's not.
Suppose the poison's just a laxative?
A jolly chemist's prank lets Romeo live.
And Juliet too. We'll obviate offending
By giving everyone a happy ending.
"Good news from Elsinore has just arrived.
The Danish royal fam'ly all survived.
And they've resuscitated dear Ophelia."
"King Lear's alive and doting on Cordelia."
"Othello's reconciled with Desdemona.
They're second-honeymooning in Verona."

BEN

I love it! A hilarious lampoon.
The ticket sales are bound to hit the moon.

CHARLOTTE

I know a way to make your coffers swell
With even greater profits.

BEN

Oh? Do tell.

CHARLOTTE

Save this burlesque till later in the season.
Six months or so from now.

BEN

Pish. For what reason?

CHARLOTTE

Strategic'ly delaying the delight
Will whet the eager public's appetite.

BEN

I see.

CHARLOTTE

And meanwhile, give them *Romeo*
From the original First Folio.

BEN

You did agree to Garrick.

CHARLOTTE

Hear my scheme.
Our fresh new parody will have more steam
If it comes after something stale and old.
Set up the joke. Then count the cash.

BEN

I'm sold.
Enact your strategy. We'll make a mint.

EDWIN

A manager is not omnipotent.
If you defy the crew, they'll mutiny.

BEN

I'll boost their pay. They'll yield their loyalty.

EDWIN

Not I. I quit. This very minute.

BEN

Stop!

EDWIN

Dost call me back?

BEN

Please leave the sword. My prop.

EDWIN

Disarmed, I go. Devoted to my art.

Edwin exits. Sallie grabs the sword.

SALLIE

Let me play Tybalt, sir. I know the part.

BEN

But can you do the fighting?

SALLIE

Yes, indeedy.

CHARLOTTE

We both took lessons from the great Macready.

Charlotte and Sallie have an elaborate sword fight.

End of play.

LIVING IN FIVE POUNDS OF SUGAR

DONNA NORMAN-CARBONE

Teaching British Literature to high school seniors has been a passion and a privilege for the past twenty years because, in it, I get to revisit, year after year, my favorite authors: the Brontës, Dickens, Shakespeare, Chaucer, Woolf, and the list goes on.

During my fifth year teaching this course, I decided to lead a tour for my students, through E.F. Educational Tours, to London and beyond to retrace the steps of some of the authors we were studying. There is no better lesson than experience.

So, my family and I, along with a colleague and her husband, set out to England with twenty-four students, most of whom had never been out of the country. We built a comprehensive tour that closely followed our curriculum to bring British literature alive.

When we arrived, we met our guide for the trip, Gus. He was a grandfatherly man whose knowledge was endless, and he had a thick, I mean thick, British accent. These students devoured every new word he taught them and so did my own children. They infused them into their own vocabulary–words like brill and gobsmacked, the loo and rucksack. Not only did it seem they were uncovering a new world, but with it came a new language, something they hadn't expected.

Gus brought us to the Tower of London where we got to see the armor worn by King Henry VIII among so many others.

My daughter, Alexa, five-years-old at the time, stopped to look at a helmet. She stared long at it, most likely the first time she'd ever seen one.

Gus noticed this and asked, "Alexa, do you know how heavy one of those is?"

Alexa shook her head.

"Well, have you ever lifted a bag of sugar?" he asked.

She shook her head again, adamantly this time, scrunching her face.

I said, "Of course you have, Alexa."

She replied in a defiant tone, "I have not."

I went on to remind her. "Every Christmas…the sugar we use to make cookies."

It was evident that Alexa was not having my explanation, so she moved on through the tower.

Later that night, as I tucked her into bed, Alexa looked at me hesitantly. I could tell she wanted to say something, but the words weren't coming easily.

"What's the matter?" I asked.

"Can I ask you a question?"

"Of course, I replied."

"Mom, when did I live in a bag of sugar?"

Surprised and confused by her question, I laughed. "You never lived in a bag of sugar," I said.

"Yes! Yes, I did. You said so today to Gus."

I sifted through the day's events to find what she was talking about and remembered the conversation about the helmet. "Oh honey, he didn't ask if you liVed in a bag of sugar. He asked if you had liFTed a bag of sugar."

I gave her a kiss goodnight. And walked away imagining her for the whole day trying to remember living in a bag of sugar.

What a sweet memory to bring home from our first trip to London. We still reminisce over that story, twenty years later.

COMING OF AGE IN SWINGING LONDON

CAROL ORANGE

Living in London during the swinging sixties opened my eyes. As a 21-year-old from a New York suburb where my father worked as a criminal defense lawyer, I'd championed the underprivileged my entire life. I was in a new marriage to Eric, my college sweetheart. He was a political science doctoral student at Princeton, and we moved to London for his graduate thesis. He wondered why so many working-class Brits voted for the Tories instead of supporting the Labour party, which seemed a more logical choice.

On the first page of the *London Times* I found an ad for "a charming bedsitting room in a Georgian townhouse on Knightsbridge's Brompton Square." Later that day, we met our landlord, Mr. Charles Brown, an architect and former RAF pilot who had been celebrated in New York after fighting in the ferocious Battle of Britain.

"I adore Americans," he said. This tall man with an infectious smile gave us the key to the furnished space on the second floor. Sitting on a velvet love seat in the living room of his ground-floor duplex, Eric and I were rendered speechless by his enthusiasm.

"Thank you, Mr. Brown," I managed to say.

Mr. Brown brought out the champagne to celebrate. We clinked glasses and shook hands. A cheque for the first month's rent was all he required.

He told us a Scottish family lived in the top-floor duplex. "They have a daughter around your age," he said as we sipped the bubbly. "Her name's Susan, and she recently graduated from the University of Geneva."

After we settled into our new digs Eric scheduled interviews with a statistical sampling of working-class Brits. I found work as a research editor on a book of Spanish art, one of several volumes in a History of Art series published by George Rainbird, Ltd. My British colleagues welcomed me, curious to know all about my American life. I, in turn, learned about their customs and language. British words seeped into my vocabulary, beginning with the "loo." At Rainbird's, the bathroom/loo was adequate, but it didn't have a radiator, and I froze when I peed during the winter. Eventually, I developed cystitis, a painful urinary tract infection that interfered with my love life. This discomfort was offset by afternoon tea when a warm-hearted Jamaican woman wheeled a trolley filled with cream puffs and scones into our editorial room.

Having majored in art history at Cornell, I couldn't believe I was paid to write about art. My advisor, Xavier de Salas, was the cultural attaché for the Spanish embassy. His eyes twinkling behind horn-rimmed glasses, he encouraged me to delve into paintings by Velazquez, El Greco and Goya. The hours flew by at the British Museum library where I found drawings by Spanish artists and gave progress reports to Señor de Salas. I will never forget his insights into "the violent nature" of Spanish art. "Our patron saint is San Sebastian," he said. "The one with all the arrows stuck into his body."

I embraced the social upheavals then erupting within England's ancient class system. I'd learned that fashion and language (accent, tone and grammar) had been telltale characteristics of class for generations, and this prejudice had economic consequences. The poetic cockney spoken by Roger and Tom, two graphic designers in our publishing company, enchanted me as much as their artistic talent. One day I stopped by their basement office and invited them to dinner. Toward the end of the evening Roger drew a whimsical sketch of our dinner and presented it to us as a gift. I was shocked by Eric's cool response during dinner and fumed after they left.

"How could they believe most working-class people can't stomach the Tories,... Mmuch less vote for them, w... When the opposite is true," he said.

"Well I guessOh, your hypothesis is more important

than being gracious!," I said, a little peeved, and decided to stay on my side of the room that night.

Based on some early interviews Eric found — much to my chagrin —many working-class people believed "their betters were born to rule."

The following day when I shared Roger's drawing with my editorial colleagues, they expressed surprise at my socializing with the lads. Their disapproval made me not like them as much and I yearned for my liberal American friends.

Damn I thought. *Great Britain still has a long way to go before becoming a true democracy.* While the *Daily Mail* called this era "the swinging sixties", the huge success of Beatles songs with their fun, racy lyrics couldn't change entrenched British habits. Yet their songs inspired a peaceful cultural revolution. Carnaby Street's bell-bottom trousers, Mary Quant's mini dresses and Vidal Sassoon's geometric haircuts became the new fashion while the Beatles paved the way for even more irreverent songs. They were the exception, their breakthrough didn't mean there was equal opportunity for everyone.

It wasn't until the Profumo Affair hit the British government— with newsboys shouting, "Minister of Foreign Affairs caught in sex ring!" that swinging London rocked. This scandal, connecting luscious call girls with at least one important Minister of State (a Tory) embarrassed the upper class no end. As "The Affair" unraveled in the British press, the Parisian *Le*

Monde featured editorials that praised Lord Profumo for "making the British more humane; more like us." Our English acquaintances told us many Londoners were titillated by the florid stories of Chelsea dinner parties, in which the upper-class host, Stephen Ward—who was responsible for introducing Christine Keeler to Lord Profumo— served dinner stark naked, except for a half apron tied around his waist. I laughed when Eric grabbed *The Daily Mail* every morning before I went off to work. It gave me hope the scandal's political implications might change his vaulted view of the Tories.

Our Brompton Square bedsitting room spread across the entire second floor, lying in the middle of the townhouse's upper and lower duplexes. A rounded archway led into a spacious living room from a square foyer. Two other doors faced the back. One door opened into a shining white kitchen, while the other door led into a large bathroom with up-to-date plumbing and an oversized bathtub. I was disappointed at the lack of a shower, until I began taking lavender and primrose bubble baths.

"You smell like an English garden," my husband teased when I emerged from the bath, my curly hair damp from the steam.

On sunny days our large room, which overlooked lush gardens, flooded with light. The flat came furnished with a Regency dining room table and chairs, a chest of drawers, two wing-backed armchairs, and two divans on either side of the room, which served as sofas by day and beds by night. Eric and I felt cozy here. The cool summer meant we never needed air conditioning.

After dinner we curled up with books on the comfortable armchairs. I devoured novels, reading Anthony Powell's masterpiece, *Dance to the Music of Time*. Powell's series of twelve novels took place between the wars, as England began to lose its hold on what was once the British Empire. The stories offered a comic examination of the British upper class's movements and manners as the main characters confronted sex, society, business and art from 1920-1940. Theirs was a small world of educated people, about to be invaded by some amazing working-class talent.

We became avid radio listeners. Our favorite program, the Saturday morning "Goon Show" with Peter Sellers of *Pink Panther* fame, provided much merriment. We used to lie side-by-side on the carpeted floor, our heads propped up by two velvet pillows from a divan so that we could listen without distractions. When one of Seller's wacky scenes erupted, we held our stomachs as we roared with laughter. Sometimes we bumped heads, which made us giggle even more.

As if this relaxed lifestyle was not wonderful enough, the cost of living in such small-scale splendor, which included dishes, silverware, and all the other items needed for light housekeeping, came to a mere 10 pounds (around $65) a week.

Eric had been spoiled by his mother's European

cuisine. "Is that what we're having for dinner?" he asked when I served sausages and beans on one of our first evenings at the flat.

Ashamed when I should have been angry, I registered for an evening course in "Continental Cooking" at the local high school. After a few sessions, where I learned how to cut an onion without crying and how to make curried lamb and rice pilaf, we could entertain up to four guests in the flat. And so my slow initiation into the pleasures of dinner parties began.

Vibrant talk about world affairs and culture swirled around our intimate room as I served three-course dinners to Eric's political acquaintances. I suppose dinner conversation must have been more engaging during the Bloomsbury era, when Vanessa and Clyde Bell and Virginia and Leonard Woolf dined with Lytton Strachey, but I had never experienced such clever repartee before. Our London crowd of twentysomethings did not claim any literary luminaries. Yet I learned how to bake Scottish salmon in its own juices from the soon-to-be famous Hugh Johnson. Hugh was a boyfriend of Liz Claridge, my art publishing colleague. Well on his way to becoming a wine connoisseur, Hugh took advantage of his Roman nose to help him distinguish the subtle bouquets of French wines. He was encyclopedic on the subject, and later committed his considerable knowledge to print. At first Hugh intimidated me with his gastronomical expertise and Saville Row suits, accessorized by a white silk handkerchief fluttering out from his lapel pocket— just so. Yet, in the kitchen, where his cheeks reddened from a warm oven, he could be as casual in his rolled-up shirtsleeves and long apron as one of the guys I grew up with in Mt. Vernon, New York.

Our Knightsbridge neighborhood contained other beautiful squares of Georgian houses, although none were quite as elegant as Brompton Square. Its unusual U shape, as opposed to the more conventional square, featured six pastel-colored Victorian houses at the bottom of the U. The interior garden was fenced in by 18th century black iron grating. Every resident had a key to the garden. There were many trees and bushes and two wooden benches in the middle. On sunny afternoons Eric sat on one of the benches as he read a book. I have a photograph of him wearing sunglasses, khaki pants and a sweater while being immersed in *On Being An English Gentlemen*. I told him his pretensions annoyed me. He may have enjoyed sharing drinks with a few of the working-class men he interviewed, but his heart and mind embraced the Tories.

"You know I'm a snob," he said, puffing on his pipe.

"You creep." I stomped to a corner of the room with crossed arms and wondered why I hadn't realized this before I married Eric. Perhaps I'd been too caught up in wedding plans to notice. Then living in London seduced me.

I spent Saturday mornings shopping on the Brompton Road, encountering a world of friendly shopkeepers— chemists, greengrocers, shoemakers, florists, butchers, publicans, and bakers. Under their tutelage I became more discerning in my selection of produce.

"If a little garden dirt still clung to its roots, and you found a wiggly worm inside, then, and only then, will you know the lettuce is fresh." Mr. Whitten, my local greengrocer advised.

It took time, but I finally overcame my American preference for vegetables wrapped in cellophane.

No one seemed to rush in this part of London. Nannies strolled in the streets as they pushed their well-dressed charges in dark blue perambulators. And at teatime, somewhere between 3:30 and 4:00 in the afternoon, most pedestrians dropped into local cafes to participate in their quaint custom. Even workmen in the street stopped digging, like clockwork, to sit down on the curb and drink tea from their thermoses.

"Hey lady... join us for a cuppa," they called to me in jest as I walked by.

I'd wave back and smile at their cheeky friendliness.

Living at #38 Brompton Square seemed like a dream. Situated in the middle of the townhouse, we traveled upstairs to the Frasers and downstairs to Mr. Brown. On some mornings, as I walked downstairs to fetch our delivered milk, I'd run into Mr. Fraser at the front door, and he'd invite us to his flat for drinks that evening. I was delighted because he concocted a superb Pimm's Cup. Although the drink was loaded with fresh fruit, its potent alcoholic content went straight to my head. On one of these occasions, Mr. Fraser asked us to call him Cameron.

While Mr. Fraser may have been the master of the cocktail, Mr. Brown was a gourmet cook. He'd leave a note on our doorstop the night before, inviting us to breakfast the next morning. "Join me for scrambled eggs and freshly-baked bread." Eric and I soon grasped our generous landlord and the restorer of more than 30 Georgian townhouses in London, had become a self-made millionaire. As our friendship developed, he confided he'd financed his architecture degree by baking cakes and bread at an all night bakery.

During the week he drove a Mini Minor to visit his work sites, to shop for veggies and fruit at Covent Garden, and just to tool around town. Until he drove us in this small car we couldn't believe he actually fit behind the wheel. On weekends he drove his Rolls Royce to his country house near Richmond. Eric and I agreed the Mini captured Mr. Brown's practical persona, which stayed true to his working-class roots, while the Rolls personified his whimsical bent, most often expressed via spontaneous gifts to others from his newfound wealth.

When we shared the occasional evening meal with him in his downstairs duplex, he regaled us with stories about his RAF experiences toward the end of the war. He also spoiled us rotten. He treated us to dinners at London restaurants where we first tasted Dover sole, and on a weekly basis he left an overflowing basket of strawberries outside our door in the morning. Mr. Brown's many indulgences made us wish we could stay in London forever.

It was a welcome surprise all our British neighbors liked us. No one commented on our accent or our preppy clothes. We were as welcome drinking beer

in a working-class pub as socializing at literary parties. We were astonished this same social acceptance didn't happen between Mr. Brown and the Frasers.

When Cameron Fraser ran into Charles Brown on the doorstep as they both fetched their morning newspapers, they would greet one another.

"Good morning, Mr. Brown," I overheard Cameron Fraser say on my way downstairs. The smell of his shaving cream permeated the narrow stairwell. If he'd been wearing his bowler, I was sure he would have tipped it.

"Good day, Mr. Fraser," Charles Brown responded, tightening the sash on his paisley bathrobe. Both men behaved as perfect gentlemen. I was befuddled they never seemed to get past social niceties.

When Eric and I dined at the Fraser flat we heard more details of the morning ritual between Mr. Fraser and Mr. Brown—how the weather, the papers and the post were mentioned. We were flattered that Barbara Fraser treated us as an extension of her family. She had led a protected life as a debutante before becoming a wife and mother so she had no special reason to welcome Americans into her midst.

The Frasers had four grown-up children, but only Susan lived at home. Eric and I often visited museums with Susan on the weekends. Sometimes she invited us to share her latest Cordon Bleu Cooking School meal. On one such night after dinner, we'd had a friendly, but heated political discussion before the conversation turned toward Mr. Brown. The Frasers admitted to being envious we Americans could easily cross a boundary that was awkward for them.

"What's he like?" Susan asked us as we helped her wash up. Of course, Eric and I spoke about Mr. Brown in glowing terms.

"Too bad we're not included in the strawberry drop," Barbara Fraser said.

When I told them Mr. Brown had asked Eric to join him on an all-expenses paid train trip in Europe, after discovering they shared a passion for steam engines, the Frasers were stunned by his generosity. "We English don't usually behave like this," Cameron said. "Good for Mr. Brown."

I admitted to feeling jealous I hadn't been asked to accompany them on this men-only trip.

Instead, I focused on the Fraser clan's generosity. They invited us to Barbara's ancestral home in Yorkshire for Christmas, and to their country place in Wales for a summer weekend where we met other family members who owned houses nearby. The Frasers didn't have much occasion to meet people outside their social milieu of hunt balls, charity events, country houses and garden parties.

I was astonished Mr. Brown's high net worth didn't bring him social connections. He made it sound like not being accepted was his choice, telling us he felt "most at home" working on construction sites with his workmen. Perhaps some reverse snobbery was at play here. However, Mr. Brown was as curious about the Frasers as they were about him. "Cameron seems a decent sort," he'd said when I answered his question about where Mr. Fraser worked.

Caught between the Upstairs and Downstairs worlds, I couldn't help thinking how much Mr. Brown and Mr. Fraser had in common, and what a pity it was they weren't friends. The two men, in their early fifties, enjoyed traveling to the Continent, and shared an appreciation for good food and wine. Both men had a delightful sense of humor and infectious laughs. Once I tried to bring them all together for a dinner at our small flat. Each party declined, making polite excuses. Eric went along with my invitation, but said he wasn't surprised when it didn't fly. I'd hoped if Mr. Brown and the Frasers could become friends it would bode well for Eric and me to resolve our political differences.

After Eric returned from the European train trip, he confessed to having an affair with an older woman he'd met on the train. Eric's betrayal pierced my heart. I have no idea what Mr. Brown was doing while Eric was getting laid, but his implicit consent made me think less of him as well.

While they were away I too transgressed, making a long call to an old boyfriend in New York. "I always loved you," I said to Jack, feeling regretful about having married Eric when I was so naive. Being alone for a week gave me strength and I realized my marriage only worked on the surface. I'd been so immersed in my wonderful job and the adventure of living in London I hadn't allowed myself to see our huge disconnect about class differences was the top layer of deeper communication problems. Two months before I'd been diagnosed with endometriosis. After my operation Eric came to visit me in the hospital. Although he brought me roses, Eric complained about my not being home to cook.

When Mr. Brown got the $250 bill for my transatlantic phone call, he asked me about it, and I had to tell him the truth. Eric was livid.

We remained in London until Princeton's fall semester was about to begin in September. Divorce was not acceptable in my family so it took me ten more years to finally end the marriage. Yet I wouldn't have missed living in London for all the world.

Education for Americans
ANNETTE TOWLER

In England, the posh people use the word Twaddle or Codswallop
The working class prefer the sound of Rubbish or Crap.

In England, the upper class have separate bedrooms with no discussion
The working class talk about it a lot and Saturday night turns into Hangover Sunday.

In jolly England, the humor is of the dry and sarcastic kind with little time for slapstick
With humor of the erotic kind, the English prefer to call it smut.

Before the dawn of Thatcher, Margaret not the occupation, and there were two groups:
Upper and lower, that is all, nothing more, nothing less between the socioeconomic status
and the English know their place.

After the Thatcher reign of terror, there were three groups:
Upper, lower and those in between who turned quite nasty when Mrs. Jones had a pond
installed in her back garden.

In England, there are several kinds of curry to eat and a favorite of the English is the
Chicken Vindaloo
Fish and Chips come a close second with roast dinners at the top of the pack.

Before the Internet, the typical British family sat down on a Sunday to curse and complain
about the weather while tucking into a big meal:
Roast Beef, Yorkshire Pudding, Brussel Sprouts, Roast Potatoes, and very thick gravy with
horseradish or Mustard on the side.

In England, the posh people use the word Twaddle or Codswallop
The working class prefer the sound of Rubbish or Crap.

The English find Americans glamorous and wonder how it feels to be a Hollywood film star, the English like the Queen.

On the subject of dating in England, the upper class mingle with their own, the middle class enjoy a glass of wine with a kiss under the mistletoe
The working class like to snog.

If invited to a wedding in England, the upper class know everyone, the middle class envy the superior wedding cake
The working class look for some other.

In England there are various interpretations of the word 'crumpet'
For some, it is delicious bread with small holes smeared with the delight of a thick knob of butter
For others it is used in the phrase 'smashing bit of crumpet' and is the American equivalent of hot.

In England, people go to church and scoff at the notion of religion
The English choose to wear their best outfits commonly referred to as Sunday best
Followed by a trip to the pub and a return home to Lamb, peas, potatoes, and mint sauce with gravy.

Among the English Upper classes, it is proper to say pardon
Among the middle classes, it is polite for the English to apologize and say I am sorry
When the English use the phrase 'excuse me' it is considered an insult flavored with sarcasm.

The English say rubber to describe an eraser and the English will laugh when they hear the phrase 'fanny pack'
Such is the humor of the common English person.
Such is the delight of being Upper, middle, or working English class.

THROUGH THE DARK

NOELLE GRASSEL

It was a dark and stormy night… no, really. London surprisingly managed to live up to many of its stereotypes within the first 3 hours that I stepped off the plane at Heathrow Airport.

It was late, about 10pm, when I snagged my oversized luggage off the baggage claim belt (which earned me plenty of looks, considering I had three tacky London-themed suitcases, courtesy of my parents). My mind was riddled with anxiety over the unfamiliar territory, people, and the fact that I embarked on this study abroad journey completely alone. I was freshly 21 and had no idea what the next five months had in store for me… let alone the next five hours!

Once I gathered my belongings, I had to find a way to my dorm. I walked over to a help desk and asked the woman behind the counter about options to Kingston University dorm halls, where she advised me that a classic red bus was the most efficient way to get there. Unfortunately she was wrong, because she gave me directions to the actual University. The dorm halls were similar to many city colleges in the states; they were basically apartments (or, as they say in London, "flats") and they were completely separate from the academic buildings. Like, blocks and blocks away separate. But that wasn't even the worst part.

The worst part was when I missed my stop on the bus. Between the heavy rain, fellow passengers, and other background noise, I didn't hear the driver when he announced the university stop. It wasn't until about 3 stops later that I mustered up the courage to ask when we'd be near Kingston, and he broke the news that we had already passed it. He was kind enough to tell me what bus to take to return that way... But I had no idea how long I would be waiting. My international cell plan hadn't kicked in yet, so I had no service and no way of looking up bus times, calling my parents, an uber, or anything.

I was on the verge of tears when I hopped off the bus and crossed the street to the other stop. If I'm being honest, I'm not quite sure how I ended up in the Mediterranean restaurant because I blacked out from the panic. Somehow, at almost midnight, I made my way to the only open establishment I could find. I walked in drenched and sobbing, asking if someone could call me a cab. Looking back on it, they probably thought I was crazy or on drugs when I first stepped in, partially because of my appearance and partially because I left my luggage right outside the door (I was so damn sick of dragging THREE suitcases all over in the pouring rain).

I got some concerned looks from the owner and what I assumed were his off-duty employees, but I was lucky. They were incredibly polite and willing to help me in any way possible. I was saved! They called me a cab, offered me food, and talked me down as I was still visibly upset. Without their help, I probably would have given up and slept at a bus stop!

But wait... that's not where the nightmare ends. My cab driver was also very kind, however, he was slightly directionally challenged, considering he kept missing the block for my dorm hall and started to insist such a road didn't exist. I felt a tsunami of relief when we figured it out and pulled up to my dorm, Clayhill Hall. That is, until I went over to the security desk, and the late-night security guard gave me a hard time about going into my room.

For context, I was a day early. But I had been in contact with the director of housing, and she assured me being a day early was not an issue. I had to embarrassingly wait to connect to Wi-Fi to show the guard my email correspondence with her. After he agreed to give me my key and directed me to my room, I thought, "This is it, FINALLY I can crawl into bed and sleep this off."

WRONG. I walked into a frowzy room without any

toilet paper or heat, AND my study abroad advisor was incorrect about one key detail... bedding. All students were told that the university provides bedding to international students, but there was a communication error between schools. When I walked in to see a bare bed, I immediately started sobbing again. I was exhausted, I felt filthy from the flight and rain, and all I kept thinking was, "I made a big mistake coming here."

Completely and utterly defeated, I unpacked some jackets, sweaters, and t-shirts to lay on and use as blankets. What else was I going to do? By then, it was well past midnight, nothing was open, and I had no idea where anything was. I barely had any idea where I was!

With the ounce of energy I had left, I used the Wi-Fi to send a quick text to my parents that I had made it, but spared them the details of my mishaps. I didn't want them to know, since I had begged for weeks for permission to go on this study abroad trip.

The good news is London became kinder to me over time. That first night was a prime example of how things couldn't get any worse. As much as it absolutely sucked having to endure that experience, I'm happy it happened. It gave me a lot to think about and reflect on, and was the push I needed to grow as a person. It changed me in the best way possible.

So, despite my first experience across the pond being one of misery, I think back on my time spent there very fondly and dream of the day I can return. Hopefully, next time around will be nothing like the first!

THE BEST LAID PLANS

JANET METZ WALTER

Sue Heller became a travel agent when she heard that Atlas Travel was looking for agents to work part-time. The hours fit her schedule as well as that of her kids, who were 11 and 9 at the time. They were now 17 and 15, and she had spent weeks planning a trip to England.

Her husband Marty was the one who encouraged her. He had caught the travel bug when he traveled out of the country to Bermuda for the first time on their honeymoon, and when they realized that Sue could get great discounts on hotels, restaurants, and even airlines, she made the decision to apply for the job.

Except for a few years hiatus when their children, Ryan and Jill, were babies, they had traveled at least once or twice a year, both in and out of the US, managing to fit in visits to Marty's parents in Florida as well.

They were known as "The Curly Family," as Sue had curly blonde hair. Marty's dark hair was not quite as curly, it was wavier. Ryan had dark hair and resembled his father, and Jill had her mother's green eyes and curly blonde hair.

Of course, the easiest thing was to simply pick a date and book a tour, but the family was much more comfortable, when possible, doing their own thing and not being tied down to hopping on the tour bus when they wanted to explore a little more, or being rushed out of a souvenir shop when they wanted to shop a little more, so Sue developed her own plan for their travel. She would spend weeks reading Fodor's and Frommers, and getting AAA guide books, to make a plan of where they would go each day. She liked using the books that she could bring with her for easy reference. Except, it didn't quite work when they planned their trip to England.

London was five hours ahead of New York, and the flight was seven hours, so they were supposed to take off at 7:30 PM and land at 7:30 AM, which was 2:30 AM New York time. The plan was to drive to Plymouth, sightseeing along the way, spend a few days exploring Cornwall, and continue North, circling back around to London, where they would spend their last few days.

Sue had asked Marty how many hours he thought he could drive on the first day, and four had seemed reasonable since they were starting out fairly early in the morning. Except... The plane took off two hours late.

Two extra hours sitting in the airport, not being able to settle down. They had planned on taking naps on the plane from about 10 until they landed. Now they didn't take off until 9:15. Dinner was served at 10. And on it went. The kids and Marty eventually slept for a few hours. Sue never slept well on planes, so she catnapped. It took almost an hour to get their rental car since everything was backed up by the plane delay. They were not thrifty packers. They had friends that brought one pair of jeans and three T-shirts for two weeks, but they packed for the "what if's" that they had experienced in their travels.

What if there was a cold spell or a heat wave? What if someone fell in the mud? That had happened. What if they decided to go to a really nice restaurant or dropped greasy food on themselves? That happened fairly often to one or the other of them.

The rental company promised that the trunk could hold four large suitcases. Not! One suitcase wound up in the back. Fortunately, the car was still large enough for two passengers in the back, but not as comfortably.

Marty was tired and irritable. He tended to lose his temper when things did not go as planned. Sue was the packer, and he accused her of packing too much. He also decided that he did not have to practice driving on the right side of the car, and the left side of the road.

Sue sat nervously on the left passenger side while Marty got right on the highway toward Winchester. The plan was to see several sights that they had read about or learned about in school that not every planned tour took people to. Sue had grown up listening to the song "Winchester Cathedral," and that was where they were headed. It was going to be a busy, whirlwind day now that they were so behind schedule.

The highways were full of roundabouts, but the signs were pretty clear, and after tackling two or three of them, Marty got used to the highway system.

It usually took Sue a while to get used to a new country, but if Winchester was a typical English town, she was already in love with England. It is actually an ancient capital and very historical. The streets were clean, the people were clean, and groups of schoolchildren in uniforms seemed happy and well-behaved. The tour books said that the crime rate is low, and it is a very safe city to visit.

The cathedral was set in a park. There were families and young couples and elderly people strolling, sitting, and playing. The cathedral itself was fairly large but by far not as ornate as the ones they had visited in Italy last year.

The custom in this cathedral was to bury people under the floor that was made up of memorial stones, now worn almost smooth and unreadable.

As they walked through the town, they came to a lovely English garden with a canal running through it, surrounded by a garden apartment complex. It seemed like an almost ideal place to live.

At 3 PM, they realized that it had been almost twelve

hours since they had last eaten. They stopped at a Mcdonald's and wound up spending almost $40 on chicken nuggets, fries and drinks. They finally found out what was not ideal about England.

They were three hours behind schedule and still had a long ride. Marty was fighting to keep awake. The time change was getting to them. He chastised Sue for planning such a long drive on the first day. Four hours had seemed reasonable if they had arrived at 7:30 AM. Sue offered to cancel the reservations in Plymouth and just find a place to stay, but Marty said to wait. Maybe he would get a second wind.

Stonehenge was somehow not as awesome as they expected. Sure, in the Outlander stories, those stones were mysterious. In their heads they had pictured women in gauzy dresses and druids dancing and praying and singing around the stones, but in reality, although one could wonder how the stones here were erected and why, it was still just a bunch of stones, not as awesome as in the stories you read about them.

Ryan decided to sit in the front with Marty for the next part of the trip.

Sue was thrilled to retreat to the back, although a little nervous about Ryan, as Marty's perception was still lacking on the left and he had almost run over a few pedestrians in Winchester, but

Ryan decided he would be more patient with him than Sue was. He was right. He quietly told him that he was about to bang mirrors with another car, rather than yelling "Watch out!" Marty did seem to get a second wind, and the drive to Plymouth was long but uneventful. They found the hotel. Dinner food and service was not great, but they were too tired to care. Sue had done a little bit of cross-packing, so they only had to bring two suitcases in. The first mistake the next day was allowing everyone to sleep late. They did not get on the road until 10 AM, and they had a long day traveling around the Cornish coast. Sue asked Marty whether they should take the faster route or the scenic one, and of course, he said scenic. They changed their schedule a bit and went ten miles out of the way to go to Falmouth because Ryan had read about a castle there.

There was a little restaurant on the grounds of the castle, so they picked up sandwiches and sodas, enough to tide them over, and wound up spending almost two hours eating and exploring. Sue bonded with Jill a little bit, over teenage things that they didn't usually discuss that much.

Pendennis Castle was a fortress built by King Henry VIII to defend the country from invasion that had breathtaking views out to sea.

Sue was in a quandary. They were only one-quarter of the way into the planned trip and she wanted to get to Tintagel, the village and castle that was the legendary birthplace of King Arthur before it closed at 6.

Sue had planned the trip to Cornwall but had not counted on all of the delays and changes to her original plan. There were so many places to see, it was stupid just to drive through all of these places without stopping to explore. Everyone was having a good time and did not seem to be in any hurry. She had no way of knowing, however, how long they really needed to spend in each place or, as it seemed, that every town seemed to close up at 6.

They drove through Penzance, the setting for the famous Gilbert and Sullivan show "The   Pirates of Penzance," and on to Land's End, at the southwestern tip of England, the last town before the ocean. They planned just to park, look at the ocean, and move on, but they found a little theme park there that the kids enjoyed, so they wound up spending about an hour there.

St. Ives is known for its famous mathematical poem, which the kids knew from their nursery rhymes. It is less known for its art galleries and museums, but it is a hilly town, and they all decided that they weren't in the mood to climb hills, so they passed through the town, looked around for a few minutes and decided to move on.

They arrived in Tintagel at about 7 PM, which was about three hours behind Sue's original plan. Once they were there, it seemed stupid not to walk to the castle, even though it was closed, as was the town itself. The castle itself is actually more of an archeological site than a castle. It was built in the 13th century and had fallen into ruin. It may have stood on the site of much earlier structures. There was a statue of the legendary King

Arthur overlooking the ocean, and a place called Merlin's Cave, which is also a tourist site.

They actually did not have to spend as much time there as Sue had thought and finally drove the remaining 62 miles to Barnstable, where they were staying that night. They arrived at 10:30. The two rooms were on opposite sides of the hotel. The only place to eat was at a greasy fish and chip place about two blocks away. They had the meals packed up and ate a greasy picnic back in the hotel.

The next day they got on the road instead of eating the expensive breakfast in the hotel. They got some snacks in a vending machine to take with them They arrived in Bristol at about 1 but it took a while to find the hotel. They finally settled into two lovely rooms less than a mile away from the road to Bath, their next destination.

They arrived in Bath at about 3, found a place in a shopping center to eat lunch, then headed to the Bath Museum.

Sue didn't think she would enjoy it that much, having seen the baths in Pompeii, but this was actually a hot spring still in existence, and she found it just as fascinating. They spent about 45 minutes at the nearby costume museum, and it was time to pick up the car before they were charged an extra $5 for overtime in the lot.

The town had been bustling when they walked to the museum, they even saw the required Native

Ecuadorian Street Band that seemed to be a fixture in almost every European city they had visited. By the time they reached the car park at 5:55, all the cars and people were gone.

They spent the early evening swimming in the hotel pool, sorry that they did not have more time to poke around Bath. They were in a pattern that found the roads were not highways, it took longer to get to every place, and every town rolled up the streets at 6. They were not morning people. They could stay up until midnight but were slow to get out in the morning, which was why they didn't like a planned tour, but this time being independent was not quite working for them, although the kids were not unhappy about relaxing at the pool

The buffet at the hotel was expensive but delicious. English food, in general, is quite bland, so they were happy to eat some well-cooked and seasoned dishes. There was a DJ in the lounge, and he picked out some great oldies that Sue and Marty enjoyed and the kids did not seem to mind.

The following day, Thursday, should not have been too difficult. They had friends who lived near York and were meeting them for dinner. They had been introduced by good friends from home. Ruby and Rhonda had been pen pals since high school, and Sue and Marty met Ruby and Sam when they came to New York to visit Rhonda and Frank. It was about a four-hour drive from Bristol to York.

It was drizzling when they left, but it started to pour about halfway through the trip, which slowed their progress.

They stopped at what they thought was a service area for lunch, but it turned out to be a truck stop in what looked like a pretty raunchy area. They bought sandwiches in the store attached to the gas station and ate in the car. They arrived by 2:30 and found their hotel near York Castle. The rain had not reached York. The castle was actually a series of buildings, including prisons, courts, and the ruins of the castle fortress, which was where they headed.

At the bottom of the place called Clifford's Tower, they looked at the 12th-century monument to 150 Jews who had been persecuted in a pogrom and had taken refuge in the castle. Rather than renouncing their religion as they were commanded, they chose to commit suicide and kill each other rather than be killed by their oppressors.

After that exhibit, they went to the Jorvik exhibit, a not-too-sophisticated Disney-type ride that showed them the plundering and eventual settling of York by the Vikings.

At 5 PM, they went into a Pizza Hut for some slices. They weren't scheduled to meet Ruby and Sam until 8:30 in case they had gotten delayed somewhere. As usual, the town was closed up. They sat in the hotel for two hours waiting for their date with Ruby and Sam.

Ryan and Jill were now at an age where they really

didn't fight a lot. Ryan was a bit of a tease, and they had silly nicknames for each other like RyRy and Jillybilly, but they did enjoy these trips and had already been to many places in the world that they knew many of their friends might never visit. They were able to handle late lunches, or no lunches, long car rides, and lots of exploring. Ryan especially liked visiting the places he read about in books or learned about in school. They became real to him. In the car, they napped or played trivia games or games on their phones. Now, sitting in the hotel, Jill pulled out the banana pouch that held the Bananagrams game, and they enjoyed playing with Sue while Marty watched the news on TV. They also had a couple of decks of cards with them, easy things to pack and use when they needed an activity.

They met Ruby and Sam at 8:30 and went to a local carvery where they had a great dinner. They enjoyed Ruby and Sam, lingered over dinner, then took a walk to a narrow pedestrian street called The Shambles. Ruby and Sam walked them back to the hotel, and they said reluctant goodbyes, not knowing when they would see each other again. It was almost midnight.

They left at about 9:30 the next morning. They spent about an hour in the Robin Hood land of Sherwood Forest, then went on to Nottingham, arriving at about 2. They found a place to eat and went on to the castle, which was now a museum. Sue had an argument with Marty and Ryan about wasting time driving to places where there was not much to see. She suggested a few

places in the Birmingham area. Marty and Ryan had
wanted to go there to find a pewter set of King Arthur
figurines that they had seen. They really had not bought
a lot of souvenirs on this trip, as they kept missing the
gift shops. Sue looked up places to visit in Birmingham,
and they rejected every place she suggested. They
finally decided to skip Birmingham.

They went on to Warwick Castle. It was huge! They
spent about two hours there visiting the wax museum
in the private quarters and exploring the castle. Sue was
getting tired of castles. They swept in and out of every
town without seeing it, but toured every castle, whether
standing or not, walking circular staircases to towers,
seeing the same armor, canopy beds, and long dining
tables. It was all starting to feel like the movie
"Groundhog Day. "

Sue wanted to see a town, poke in and out of shops,
and get the feel of the streets of Notting ham, which was
much bigger than they thought it would be. Marty's
answer was that everything was outrageously priced,
and in Europe, you visited castles and palaces because
those were not major attractions in the US. Besides, they
had no time to see the cities because he was doing so
much driving. Sue began to regret spending so much
time planning this trip. She figured it would have been
easier to just hop on a tour and put up with the
restrictions. At least everything wouldn't be her fault,
but she knew that everything that went wrong would be
her fault no matter what. They had no choice but to

continue going. They were used to being able to browse through tourist towns at night. This was just weird.

They arrived at Stratford-Upon-Avon at about 6. They rode around looking for the hotel. They finally found the bridge that they were looking for to get there.

The town was pretty, and although they figured everything would be closed, they decided to take a walk anyway.

The area surrounding the river was charming, and they enjoyed their walk. They came to a shopping area that they assumed would be closed, but there was a souvenir shop that was open. Jill bought a bottle opener to give as a gift to a friend. Sue found earrings that she liked. All of the shops had sale signs, and Sue knew that she wanted to come back the next day. Marty and Ryan were annoyed. They wanted to push on to Oxford and finally London. Sue couldn't figure out what was wrong with them. They always collected souvenirs or T-shirts everywhere they went and loved browsing in the shops. Sue did not cave in this time. She did not plan to be in London until late afternoon.

They ate dinner in the hotel that had special rates for kids. It was the cheapest hotel meal they had had on the trip. They took a walk around the hotel and stayed up late watching a movie. Marty decided that Sue and Jill would shop the next morning, and he and Ryan would sleep in, but Sue woke him with the hair dryer. He got up but refused to go shopping. Jill and Sue went into town, but now their hearts weren't in it because they were made to feel so guilty about wanting to stay. They poked in and out of a few stores, looking for a shop they had seen the night before when they ran into Marty and Ryan. They had already checked out the shop and had not bought anything. They went back to the hotel for breakfast, and almost immediately after breakfast, Ryan got sick with cramps and nausea. They assumed it was food poisoning. When he felt a little better, they got into the car to drive to Oxford, and Ryan told Sue that she would be the navigator for the day, which made them realize that he really didn't feel well. Sue gave him some medication that she had for an upset stomach, and he went to sleep in the back. As they approached Oxford, Ryan woke up and said he felt better.

Oxford was disappointing to Ryan because it was a real city college with no campus, just buildings scattered around the city. It was also drizzling, so they bought Ryan an Oxford T-shirt and headed back to the car. To their surprise, the streets were like 5th Avenue at Christmastime. Throngs of people were strolling around, and it was difficult to get past them.

They made it to London at about 3:30 and found the hotel fairly easily. But nothing else was easy. They were given a room with two single beds, a cot and a pull-out couch, and no shower head on the handheld shower. They said they would move them the next day. Sue started to call other hotels, and they came back and offered them two rooms for the same price. After some negotiating, they wound up with a double and a twin next to each other, and they adopted Jill's philosophy of the month "We'll deal with it."

They took advantage of a laundromat around the corner, as they were starting to run low on underwear and socks, glad that they did not have to wash things out by hand that might not dry by morning.

The concierge pointed the way to some nearby restaurants, and they did what they called "The Restaurant Walk," comparing menus and prices until they picked the Italian place. Afterward, they were actually able to walk around the area. Finally, they were in a real city, similar to New York, where the people dressed more like city people. The women wore jeans, slacks, or business suits, heels, and makeup. In the small cities and towns they had visited, there was no reason to be that dressed up or wear makeup. They were much more casual.

The next day was Sunday. They got to Buckingham Palace an hour before the changing of the guard, and they still couldn't get a spot at the fence. Sue found a spot on the side where she and Jill were only two deep instead of four deep where Marty and Ryan were standing, but it was still hard to see. It was a boring hour of waiting, and after the first ten exciting minutes, just to be there watching this world-renowned ceremony was just as boring. Jill got a spot at the fence when people got bored and started to walk away.

The guard came in with much pomp and circumstance, then individuals just walked back and forth for the next half hour. When it was over, the family walked to Westminster Abby through St James Park, and after touring the Abby, they found a place to eat. Jill bought a T-shirt and they took the train to the Tower Of London.

They had a great Beefeater guide who was very enjoyable. They saw the crown jewels and heard about every execution that took place there, including Anne Boleyn, Becket, and a few others. They then took a train back to Picadilly Circus and wandered around the Times Square of London. They came upon the Chinatown of Soho, where they found a place to eat. The food was a little different than what they were used to, and Jill wasn't happy because she didn't love Chinese food to begin with.

The next morning they headed for Windsor Castle. They soon found out that it would have been easier to go by train, as the drive through the city was kind of difficult from where they were.

Windsor Castle stretched on for blocks, but the only exhibits that were open to the public were Queen Mary's Doll House and the State Public rooms. They learned a little history of the castle and the monarchs that lived there. As they were leaving, they walked through an alley and happened upon a gift shop that had the best prices they had seen on the Tudor Mint pieces that they had spent the whole vacation looking for. The owner was lovely and reminded them of Ruby in looks and personality. They wound up spending an hour there. From a few small souvenirs, they wound up spending about $500 for one large piece depicting wizards and druids around a dragon and five or six smaller pieces, all containing round color-changing crystals. They had a place for the display at home. Marty's attitude was that he would rather buy them and possibly use some of the smaller ones as gifts than be sorry that they hadn't bought them. They had finally hit pay dirt, and it was worth the wait. They were all very excited.

The next day was their last day. There were still some places they wanted to see, and they decided to play it by ear and see how it went.

They started out at Harrods, curious to see what all the talk about this store was. As they walked around, they knew. Every display in the store was set up in an appealing and attractive fashion. There was even a candy department with every kind of candy and truffle imaginable set up in beautiful display cases. They found colorful marzipan and some butter fudge that they bought. In another display, they found their favorite meringues. There was a food department displaying fruit from all over the world, and whole fish lying side by side in a showcase.

Jill wanted to see the toy department. There were people up there demonstrating toys that climbed walls and made hats out of plastic bubbles. There were kid-sized gas-powered cars for $30,000. The stuffed animals were spilling out of a huge Noah's Ark.

It was raining when they got out. They had plans to go see a show, but most of the shows they were interested in were sold out at the half-price ticket booth. They were not that upset,

knowing that they could see most of the same shows in New York. They decided instead to take a train to find the Hard Rock Cafe to get T-shirts for the kids to add to a growing collection from all over the world. They then took another train to Hyde Park to see a London residential neighborhood. It was quite upscale and different from the middle of the city.

Their last stop of the day was Covent Garden, the fashion and culture district of London. They walked around a bit but didn't stay long. They were happy that after all of their difficulties and aggravation on the trip that their last day was enjoyable and relaxing. They had missed the British Museum, but they felt that they probably had more fun in Harrods.

They got back to their hotel and collapsed for a few hours before dinner. They found a great restaurant a little farther down the block than they had ever walked before. They spent some time poking around a gift shop for some last-minute gifts, and came back to the hotel to pack, pretty sure that it would not be their last trip to London.

The Crow at the Tower of London

Mahjabeen Haider

The black crow knew
With the wind of change
Blew
The black crow knew
When Henry's plague
Decided to invade
Creating a mental raid
The black crow knew
When the death bell rang
From Anne Boleyn's neck
Her voice no longer sang

The black crow knew
When the sweat and plague
Attacked the streets
King Henry did not live
To hear the patter of many tiny feet
The black crow knew
The kingdom of doom
With lockdown 2020
London became haunted
City of isolated gloom
The black crow knew
Observing from the tower
Fear the black crow
Of London city
Their freedom and powers

TRAVELOGUE – LONDON, ENGLAND – NOVEMBER, 1997

STEPHEN J. DEWOLF

I had been to London on previous occasions in the late '70s and early '80s as a U.S. employee of a U.K. software company. Those trips were short and work-intensive, consisting of work, restaurant/pub/room service, and did not leave much time or energy for exploring, as my flights east were typically on Sunday nights and then leaving on Friday afternoons.

This trip, as an independent IT contractor working on behalf of an international bank, was to be longer, spanning 2+ weeks, including weekends. I was looking forward to working with new people and having time to explore the city.

My trip was very different from my earlier trips in several ways, and that I was 15 years older granted me a new perspective on the people, the culture, the architecture—and the food.

The locals were uniformly pleasant, and some were amused at this "Yankee colonial" in awe of what the natives just took for granted. They loved to hear and answer my many questions–lucky for me–and I learned much more from the Q&A than I would have strolling solo and aloof.

I will describe the trip in three parts: my first week, the rest of my stay, and my return flight home.

PART 1 ` - MY FIRST WEEK: "SAD SONGS (SAY SO MUCH)"

(Not yet Sir) Elton John recorded "Candle in the Wind" in 1984. Often thought to have been a fan of Marilyn Monroe, the song was meant as a more general tribute to famous people who died too soon. He could not have known …

On the eve of my flight to London, Princess Diana died in a car crash in Paris.

The weather when I arrived was pleasant, the sky mostly cloudy, but the atmosphere in the city was considerably darker, with nothing to do with smog.

I was a teenager when President Kennedy was assassinated in Dallas in 1963 (and when Robert Kennedy and Martin Luther King were assassinated in Los Angeles and Memphis, respectively, in 1968). I was certainly saddened but had little appreciation for the wider impact of JFK's death. Even with the stately funeral procession along the wide Pennsylvania Avenue to Arlington National Cemetery, it seemed somewhat remote, sort of "there".

London that week had a totally different feel. Diana had been born to privilege and had been married to the future king of England and bore him two heirs before they divorced, but her charm, humor, and her humanitarian efforts endeared her to all Brits and much of the world. The Londoners not only loved Diana but also clearly treated her as one of "theirs" and felt a great loss. Even as a visitor, I couldn't help but feel the same. The pall over the city affected everybody, and work was still getting done but much more slowly.

Despite Diana's divorce from Prince Charles, she was granted a royal funeral. The funeral procession passed along what were relatively narrow streets lined several deep with mourning people of all ages. I watched on television in a pub and did not notice the relatively shocking breach of royal protocol - or, perhaps, just a sincere sign of respect - in which Queen Elizabeth bowed her head as the casket passed in front of her. My wife at home did notice it, however. The press and gossipers made as much of this as they did of the fact that the royals did not return from Balmoral Castle immediately after Diana's death was announced. Protocol has always been more closely watched in the U.K. than here in the U.S., but the intrusiveness of reporters, photographers, and commentators was then and remains just as intense, unfortunately.

Westminster Abbey was packed with royal and other

famous mourners. Much has been written about the sermons and speeches; you know where to find them.

I admit that among this very solemn service, the most emotional part for me was Elton John sitting at a piano and singing, for the first and apparently only time live, a newly written version of "Candle in the Wind" specifically for Princess Diana entitled "Goodbye, England's Rose." With but one day to rehearse the performance of the new lyrics in the Abbey, and then performing for such an audience frankly blew me away. I listened again today while writing this piece, and my eyeglasses were well-moistened from the inside.

Diana's final journey and burial on the Spencer estate concluded a day and a week where it did seem at times that time stood still, and everyone took time to reflect.

PART 2- THE REST OF MY STAY IN LONDON: "ENGLAND SWINGS LIKE A PENDULUM DO"

With some evenings free as well as a long weekend, I was able to get "out and about" and see sights I had only read about or seen in pictures or movies. Here are some points of interest—and interesting points, not in any order.

Porter's English Restaurant in Covent Garden (central London). OK, so food came first! I went with a colleague for dinner. I've never been much of a foodie, but I admit I was put off by such menu items as spotted dick and steak & kidney pudding (pie). I think I had Shepherd's Pie as an entrée ad then tried Steamed Syrup Sponge for dessert. Wow! A simple sponge cake slathered with a sauce made from Golden Syrup. It turns out that this dessert was a common dish for boys in public (we call it "private") school, but for me it was special. I later purchased some Golden Syrup to take home.

Blackfriars Pub. Located in the "City," Blackfriars was an old-fashioned tavern with typical English pub fare, several beer and ale choices, a dart board, and apparently lots of regulars.

Big Ben. Its image in countless photographs and movies might make it the most famous clock tower in the world, but "Big Ben" is actually the nickname for the largest of five bells in what is now called the Elizabeth Tower. The smaller bells toll the quarter-hours, while Big Ben tolls the hours. I could hear the gong from quite a distance, but when I walked past the tower at the top of the hour, the "gong" was more like a "GONGGGG!"; and it seemed I was feeling the sound as well as hearing it.

221B Baker Street. I was and am a fan of the Sherlock Holmes mysteries without having solved any of them myself. The taxi driver chuckled when I gave him this address (more on taxis to follow) because, of course, he knew there was no such address on Baker Street. I didn't see any Baker Street Irregulars, either. Oh, well, I then took a short walk to …

Madame Tussaud's Wax Museum. Suffice it to say I was like a child the way I literally gaped at the faces of the decorated wax figures, staring and waiting for one of them to move or even twitch or blink. They really did look so real.

London Underground. The key word is "underground," with several stations up to (or "down to") more than 150 feet below street level. Locally called the "Tube," the nearly 300 stations are arched like tubes, as are the entrances to the tunnels between stations. Directions to the exits are signed "This Way Out" with an arrow. I thought the signs should say "This Way Up", and the escalator rides to the surface were in some cases, quite daunting. The train cars seemed small, but there always seemed to be room at least to stand, even in busy times.

Surface transport was just as interesting, with red double-decker buses and black taxis. I rode once on the top level of a bus and felt like I was on a parade float cruising the street. The diesel taxis are deceptively large. Stepping into such a taxi is like entering a magical tent in a Harry Potter movie. The cab looks small from the curb (or "kerb"), but as a sole passenger, I felt I was in a limousine. Licensed drivers must pass a test called "the knowledge" and have to answer questions about the quickest way to get from one location to another. It can take years for an aspiring driver, using his personal means of travel, to become familiar with the more than 20,000 streets in the greater London area. One especially talkative driver was as proud of his wife and parents for financing his 2 ½-year quest as he was of his accomplishment.

St. Paul's Cathedral. After the original structure was destroyed in London's Great Fire of 1666, the current cathedral was built over 35 years, from 1675 to 1710. It doesn't look that old. It is imposing in size though still smaller than St. Peter's Basilica in Rome but is still glorious outside and inside.

PART 3: "UP, UP, AND AWAY"

It was time to return home, not "ín my beautiful balloon" but on a Virgin Atlantic 747 whose "Upper Class" seats were the same as British Airways first class seats but priced at business class in B.A. and other airlines. It was my first time traveling in first class, and the trip was certainly first class. Thank you, (then soon to be) Sir Richard Branson.

Once we reached cruising altitude, the captain announced a poetry contest with the subject being Virgin Atlantic itself. The prize was to be a magnum of champagne. I am not a drinker, but why not give it a go? The very slightly modified (or "tarted up") version follows.

I was disappointed to hear that I did not win the contest, but two of the cabin crew appeared before we were on the final approach and said they loved my poem and wanted to include it in an issue of the company newsletter. They then provided a big box of assorted Belgian chocolates. Wow! It was I could do to bring the box home unopened.

A car ride home and the trip became a good memory. I looked forward to the next of several return trips for this project, both to London and to Poole on England's south coast, and as my passport page shows, I did.

My first week did not fit the stereotype of "Jolly Old England." It was certainly not "jolly."

As for "Old", while I felt architecture in London was so old it should be spelled "olde," my Brit colleagues told me to check out a 1000-year-old church and the even more ancient monoliths of Stonehenge. Next time(s), for sure!

Perhaps it was not so much that I perceived England as old as it is that compared to England, the United States will always be young!

The Virgin Atlantic Experience

Stephen J. deWolfe

There are hundreds of places to which people fly,
And almost as many are their reasons why.
For business, pleasure, or if the two they're mergin'
Many thousands of flyers have chosen Virgin.

Their first reason is the way they get a ticket;
Some airlines make this process seem like a thicket.
"Every passenger's important," all airlines say,
But on flight after flight, Virgin treats you that way.

At most airports, drab colors prevail left and right,
But Virgin stands out with its colors red and white.
It's not just bright colors, though, it's also bright smiles
That send you on your journey of thousands of miles.

For any flight at all, no one wants to leave late.
Virgin's planes are on time when they pull back from the gate.
Pre-flight's are performed, then the plane's declared ready;
Wait time is kept short; take-offs are smooth and steady.

The comfort continues once the plane's in the air;
The seat pocket's well-filled, and the food is good fare.
If you need pillows, blankets or the latest news
Or food, snacks or drinks, just ask the great cabin crews.

They show you safety procedures and serve you food,
And they do what they can to maintain your good mood.
The flight may be full, but they show great persistence
In providing top-flight passenger assistance.

Though flights are diverted to avoid severe storms,
They're well scheduled, with on-time arrivals the norms.
The crew on the flight deck work quite well together
From take-offs to landings in all kinds of weather.

But there's more to Virgin than cabin and flight crew;
There's an army of others with tough tasks to do
In that schedule segment known as "turnaround times"
Between the soft touchdowns and the very smooth climbs.

There's no ticketing hassle when the flight's well-booked;
The bags are loaded quickly; the meals are well-cooked;
The planes are well-kept by senior maintenance crews
With years of experience; they've all paid their dues.

When each passenger leaves for his city or town,
No one's job is completed when the plane's tied down.
For the airline to grow, staff take part in a movement
To hone new techniques for the airline's improvement.

The sign of how thoroughly each employee trains
Is that the owner is seen to ride his own planes.
But Richard Branson's seat is just like all the rest;
On every Virgin flight, you're treated like his guest.

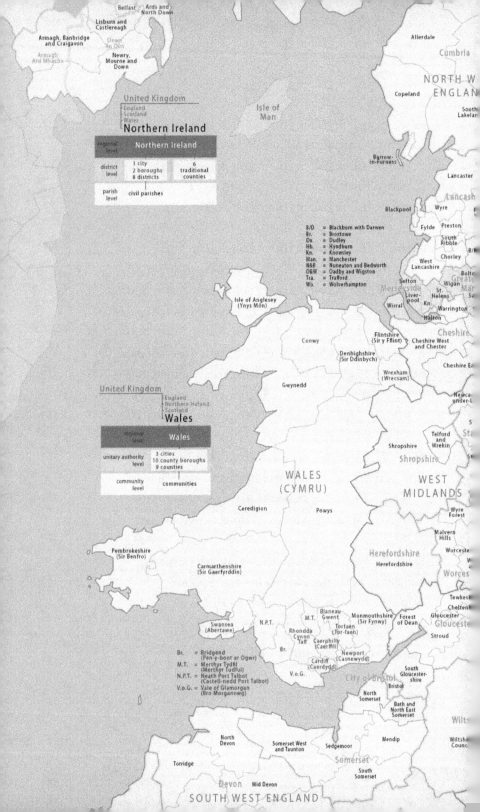

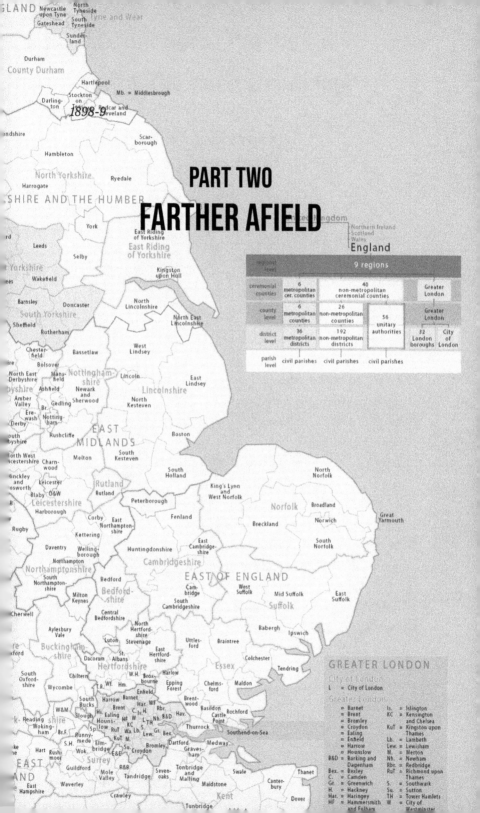

PART TWO
FARTHER AFIELD

England

region level			9 regions				
ceremonial counties	6 metropolitan cer. counties		40 non-metropolitan ceremonial counties			Greater London	
county level	6 metropolitan counties	26 non-metropolitan counties		56 unitary authorities		Greater London	
district level	36 metropolitan districts	192 non-metropolitan districts				32 London boroughs	City of London
parish level	civil parishes	civil parishes		civil parishes			

GREATER LONDON
City of London
L = City of London

Greater London
= Barnet   Is. = Islington
= Brent   KC = Kensington
= Bromley   and Chelsea
= Croydon   KuT = Kingston upon
= Ealing   Thames
= Enfield   Lb. = Lambeth
= Harrow   Lew. = Lewisham
= Hounslow   M. = Merton
B&D = Barking and   Nh. = Newham
      Dagenham   Rbr. = Redbridge
Bex. = Bexley   RuT = Richmond upon
C. = Camden   Thames
Gr. = Greenwich   S. = Southwark
H. = Hackney   Su. = Sutton
Har. = Haringey   TH = Tower Hamlets
HF = Hammersmith   W = City of
     and Fulham   Westminster

Doughnuts @ Brighton Pier

KATHRYN COCKRILL

Hurried along wooden boards
with the sea rolling beneath our feet,
insistent that the best doughnuts
are at the end of the pier
(despite every doughnut stand being the same.)

The world spins around us,
the rides on the boardwalk lighting up the sky,
the grey sea foaming underneath,
extending as far as the eye can see
dropping into the horizon
as if we're standing at the end of the Earth.

Doughnuts in hand, we hurry back
avoiding the planks about to give way,
bent and buckled from years of traffic,
stepping off of the pier and down onto the beach,
our feet sinking into the stones
stumbling like new-born fawns
the waves laughing with pebble-framed mouths.

Eventually, we sink into the pebbles
legs aching from the long-walked battle,
looking out across the water,
the waves frothing at our feet
encircled by seagulls
with their eager eyes sizing up the treats,
frantically covered by a white paper bag,
grease spots leaking through.

Then, the first bite,
hot, crispy shells with soft, fluffy dough underneath,
sugar-coated lips smiling as we rush to eat them all
before the seagulls make their move.

We crumple up the bag and throw it away,
sliding along the stones, laughing as we make our way back
off of the beach, away from the pier,
back into concrete streets and graffiti-stained buildings,
back into the dreary mess of it all
but still with sugar coated lips smiling
from that little taste of home.

HAPPY CHRISTMAS: THE TIMELESS CHARM OF THE HOLIDAY SEASON IN ENGLAND

DAVID LANGE

I have many happy memories of time spent in England, but my fondest memories have to be enjoying the beauty and charm of the holiday season. As an Air Force officer assigned in the United Kingdom, I had the pleasure of experiencing three Christmases in England. There was a certain Old-World beauty to the experience that set it apart from my holiday experiences in the United States. Also, there seemed to be less commercialism and fanfare associated with the holidays. They were more like I felt Christmas should be —joyous yet reverent and respectful. England is situated above 50 degrees north (Alaska is the only U.S. state farther north), and the winter days are very short. Near Christmas, there were less than eight hours of daylight each day. Add in the typical thick cloud deck above and you have a somewhat somber setting reminiscent of a

Dickens novel. For all this, there was plenty of holiday cheer to brighten the days. I'd like to share just a few memories.

THE SANTA TRAIN

If you enjoyed The Polar Express or got excited watching Harry Potter and friends zipping along the tracks on the Hogwarts Express, then you'll likely love one of Britain's holiday train experiences as much as my family and I did. Our journey was taken on the Nene Valley Railway with a lovely old steam engine pulling us across the English countryside from Wansford Station to Peterborough and back. We were fortunate enough to experience the journey while there was snow on the ground. Father Christmas (Santa) greeted all the arriving children before the ride and each child was presented with an age-appropriate gift. Upon the ride itself, traditional holiday treats were provided to all guests. The fare included complimentary drinks (hot chocolate, warm apple cider, and soft drinks or an alcoholic beverage for adults), a bag of holiday sweets for the kids, and a tasty traditional mince pie for each guest.

As we traveled the lovely British countryside, Father Christmas made his way through the train and sat with each and every child. It was a very lovely experience. After the ride, we enjoyed looking around the yard and checking out all the old trains which included a Thomas the Tank Engine special engine. Before leaving, we took photos by the wonderful traditional red British phone booth.

PANTOMIME

I think my wife and I loved this as much as our two small children did. I had never experienced anything quite like it before. A pantomime is a very special form of participatory theater production where the audience is not only encouraged, but absolutely expected to participate in the action. The productions spring up around England during the holiday season and often have famous personalities playing some of the roles. The sets are an explosion of brilliant colors and the costumes are no less spectacular. The scores are brilliantly crafted and often set to very catchy familiar tunes. The performances are chock full of clever slapstick comedy bits, as well. The pantomimes very frequently retell well known fairy tales. The show I took my family to see in 1999 was a retelling of Jack and the Beanstalk. The performance was staged in the lovely Theatre Royal in Bury St. Edmunds. I think we smiled and laughed through the entire production. I can still see the image of a dozen adorable little children, dressed as spiders, dancing about the stage as the music from ABBA's "Money, Money, Money" accompanied the movement. The audience participation aspect of the show was truly a riot. As an example, a villain might try to frighten the hero by saying "I'm going to get you, Jack." The main character would respond "Oh no you're not." The villain would double-down and shout back "Oh yes I am!" At this point, the audience would know the game was on and would shout back from the seats "Oh no you're not" … and the argument would volley back and forth like some hilarious tennis match until the villain would give up the fight and cast an angry glance toward the audience who was clearly siding with the hero.   The interactions were always delightfully entertaining. My one regret is that I did not attend more pantomimes during my time in England. Pantomime plays are a wonderful tradition whose legacy dates back many, many centuries.

HOLIDAY MARKETS AND LOCAL EVENTS

Not unlike in other European countries, a variety of wonderful holiday markets would spring up around England during this festive time of year. Unique gifts and consumables were made available for customers looking for the perfect holiday gift or treat. Each event would have a local flavor and you were sure to find treasures unavailable in any retail store. Beyond the shopping, many towns had their own traditions and festivals that date back long before any of the current residents were born. You were never quite sure what to expect. While living in England, my rented home was situated on a winding country road between two villages. We'd frequently have horseback riders trot by; the horse and riders' heads bouncing above the hedgerow that formed a barrier between our property and the street. On one Christmas Eve, I remember calling my son to the window so that he might see Father Christmas, himself, as he passed by our home, waving to us, from a horse-drawn cart. A number of towns also have beautiful churches and the services held in medieval stone cathedrals are a true spectacle to behold. Stone walls, illuminated by the flickering candlelight, reverberated with the forceful and well-articulated words of seasoned clergymen and the harmonious hymns sung by the choir.

TELEVISION

Even upon the "Tele," the British Broadcasting Corporation, or more familiarly the "BBC," would broadcast special holiday shows. These shows seemed more set upon filling our hearts with the spirit of the holiday than on acting as some marketing ploy to sell products. I remember first seeing the animated short film, "The Snowman," on BBC 4 from our small cottage in England. This beautiful film is without dialog yet relies upon stunning graphical content and a beautiful score to tell a heartwarming story about love and loss set within the context of a young boy's magical encounter with a snowman he crafts on Christmas Eve. To this day, I have watched "The Snowman" every year as part of the run-up to Christmas.

THE STREETS OF LONDON

While, thankfully, not as soot-covered as the Industrial Age London portrayed in Charles Dickens' works, a trip into the capital city is a holiday must. The holiday hustle and bustle of the big city stands in stark contrast to the tranquil expressions of the holiday in more remote villages but is no less a part of the Christmas experience in England. I'd try to make it into London at least once during the season just to absorb the festive holiday lights and decorations and immerse myself in the human tide of holiday energy. It may not be for everyone but its certainly an experience I'd recommend for most.

THE CLOCK

One of my last beautiful holiday memories from England relates more to New Year's Day than to Christmas. For years I had drooled over the beautiful grandfather clocks I saw in shop windows. When I moved to England, there was actually a shop on my base that specialized in selling these beautiful clocks— all made by hand in Germany. After much handwringing, I finally decided to part with several thousand of my hard-earned dollars to order my favorite. The clock itself would be customized to my specifications and then delivered to my residence. The *timing* of my decision was not without significance. In fact, it was tremendously significant. The year was 1999 and my desire was to have my new clock in time to ring in the new year—2000. On December 16th, two burly Germans came knocking at my door. They looked exactly like the frightening characters I had seen in a number of Viking movies over the years. The two deliverymen didn't speak a word of English and had driven my beautiful clock through the Chunnel (connecting the European mainland with England) only that morning. With German precision, they set up my timepiece while my 11-month-old daughter looked on in horror. They were pretty fierce looking characters. With the clock in place, and precisely set as only a navigator could ensure, we were ready for New Year's Eve. We tuned our television to BBC and watched as the clock ticked down. My grandfather clock was set to play the Westminster chimes, the same tune played by Big Ben. As the new year was born, my heart soared as my grandfather clock chimed in exact sequence with Big Ben on the tele. It's my wish that, one day, my little princess (my oldest daughter was born in England) will inherit that clock that welcomed the year 2000 for her first New Year's celebration.

I have so many special holiday memories from England but I hope that the stories I chose to share will encourage you to take a trip across the sea to experience the beauty and grandeur of the holiday season in the United Kingdom. In England, they don't say "Merry Christmas," they wish each other a "Happy Christmas." My Christmases in England were very happy.

On This Spot

Linda Trott Dickman

For the Jews of York, R.K.

Just over 200 miles from London,
like an incessant clock,
banging at intervals
it came. First the calls, deep low
grumbling, growing louder, angrier.
The hundred fifty of us resolved to
keep our faith.

We have been inside the castle walls
for a week now, praying that Jehovah
strengthen them
with as much spirit as He toppled Jericho's.

Their trumpet? A siege engine,
built of debt,
Malebisse's fuel.
Benedict gone, his widow and children murdered,
we sit, faith stronger than our hunger
on this Shabbat HaGadol,
knowing that our blood will be spilled on the lentils.

Our Passover is nigh,
Hear O Israel!
Here, O Israel.
We will not deny You.

MARITIME BRITAIN

DAVID LANGE

I had barely arrived in England before I began reading Patrick O'Brian's magnificent Aubrey-Maturin series of sea novels set in 19th Century England and, indeed, around the globe. A lifetime lover of all things nautical, I was readily willing to believe my mother's tales of there being a sea captain in my bloodline somewhere back in the foggy past of yesteryear. The aforementioned novels vividly detailed the adventures of the two friends, Jack Aubrey and Stephen Maturin, as they progressed through a never-ending series of adventures while serving in the Royal Navy. The locations described were not a world away but, instead, just a short train ride into London. Beyond my fascination with the facts behind the fiction, I was also enthusiastic to learn more about the challenges of navigation during this period, more so because I was an Air Force navigator, by profession.

Dava Sobel's wonderful book, *Longitude*, detailed the amazing tale of John Harrison, a British clockmaker. He solved a challenge that had been perplexing the Royal Navy for as long as it had been in existence—how to determine longitude while at sea. The book details his 40-year quest to create the perfect chronometer for use at sea. These two books, and the places and artifacts described within, set the stage for two wonderful trips in England. The first trip was a day trip to Greenwich, in London, and the second trip was a two-day visit to Portsmouth, about 70 miles southwest of London.

On February 14, 1998, I decided the time was right to take my family to visit the Old Royal Observatory at Greenwich in London. Greenwich is a very special place for a number of reasons. For starters, it's located right on the Prime Meridian (0 degrees longitude) and it's also where time starts (world time zones are measured as either plus or minus hours from Greenwich Mean Time, or GMT). There are several ways to get to London but once you're there, I recommend making your way to Charring Cross station from wherever your starting point is. Near Charring Cross is a dock where you can book passage on a number of Thames River cruises. Several of these take you to Greenwich and back. If you're not into river cruises, you can get the Docklands Light Railway from Tower Hill which will also take you to Greenwich. Seeing as how my goal was to enjoy a nautical-themed day, a one-hour narrated cruise down the famous Thames was a perfect way to start the adventure. Along the way, sites of interest were discussed in a clever and entertaining fashion with a typical British flair.

One of the first spectacles to greet you as you depart your boat at Greenwich is the magnificent *Cutty Sark*. The *Cutty Sark* is a ship so famous that they named a whiskey after it. Built in Scotland in 1869, the *Cutty Sark* was one of the fastest of the famed "clipper" ships; beautiful state of the art sailing vessels that regularly made cargo runs around the globe. The advent of steam powered vessels eventually spelled the downfall for these beautiful tall ships but, at the time, they represented the pinnacle of sailing technology.

Once you're done checking out the Cutty Sark, the next stop on this day trip is a visit to the Old Observatory and Museum. On your way, should you like a break, there's a beautiful park at the foot of the Observatory which is a great place for picnics or to let the little folk run wild. There are also lots of great shops in the area if you want to spend some money on a unique shopping extravaganza.

The Observatory itself is on top of a hill and is filled with great exhibits relating to the history of navigation. The Greenwich Meridian is also conspicuously marked, as befits a noteworthy tourist attraction. Of course, you'll want to have your photo taken straddling the line on the ground, with one foot in the Eastern Hemisphere and the other in the Western Hemisphere, while the atomic clock behind you provides a highly accurate read-out of the precise time of your visit. It may sound a bit gimmicky but it you reflect upon the history; you'll have an extra level of appreciation for the significance of the moment. And, if nothing else, it's a pretty good place to adjust the time on your personal watch.

I entered the Old Observatory and Museum with a sense of reverence, as if I were visiting a cathedral. I stood in awe as I saw John Harrison's original H-1 clock (his first try), H-2, H-3, and the final prize-winning H-4 chronometer on display. As previously described, you'll have a much greater appreciation for these remarkable devices and John Harrison's genius if you read Dava Sobel's *Longitude* before you visit.

Beyond the Old Observatory and Museum, there's another "must-see" stop while you're at Greenwich and that's the National Maritime Museum. The Museum is filled with all kinds of interesting historical artifacts and artwork but it also has a really fun interactive kids' room with lots of exciting hands-on gadgets for the younger sailors in your party to fidget with. The Museum's collection houses more than two-million items and there's no place like it in the world. If you're a fan of Britain's maritime history, be sure you block out enough time to explore the museum's impressive collections.

After our visit to the Museum, we made our way

back to the dock where return boats departed on the hour. While the narration was similar to that provided on the way down river, you may find the voyage even more enchanting after the sun has set. St. Paul's Cathedral, Big Ben, the Tower Bridge, and the Tower of London are just a few of the sites you'll see along the way.

With my feet wet, so to speak, I was thirsty to explore more of England's maritime history and one of the best places to visit is Portsmouth. There are several ways to get there. We drove from home but, if you're basing out of London, you can take a train down to Portsmouth. It's about a ninety-minute train ride. While there, we stayed at the beautiful old "Queen's Hotel," which was just a short walk from all the historic locations we wanted to visit. First on my list was the famous *HMS Victory*. *Victory* was Admiral Horatio Nelson's flagship during the famous Battle of Trafalgar. Nelson is, perhaps, the most famous character in all the world's naval history. If you are familiar with Trafalgar Square in London, then you have no doubt seen Nelson's column, one of London's most famous monuments. The monument was erected as a measure of the great esteem Lord Nelson was held in by an entire nation indebted to his service. The Battle of Trafalgar took place on October 21, 1805 and pitted the British Royal Navy against the combined fleets of France and Spain. French leader, Napoleon Bonaparte, had

aspirations to invade and conquer England. His Grande
Armée (or "Grand Army") was more than capable of
overwhelming the British Army. There was one small
catch, Napoleon had to find a way to traverse the
twenty some-odd miles of the English Channel that
separated England from the European mainland.
Standing between him and his goal was the formidable
Royal Navy. To ensure a safe passage, Napoleon knew
he'd have to eliminate the threat. And thus, the stage
was set for one of the greatest naval battles in the
history of the world. The engagement took place off the
coast of Spain. Leading his fleet from the front and
outnumbered 33 to 27 ships, Nelson led the Royal Navy
to its greatest victory, thus saving the island nation. The
combined French and Spanish fleet lost 22 ships while
the Royal Navy did not lose a single vessel. Though
brutally battered, HMS Victory refused to yield. Lord
Nelson lost his life to a sniper's bullet during the
engagement and a brass plaque marks the spot where
he fell onboard Victory. He gave his last full measure
and won a victory that truly shaped world history.

Once in Portsmouth, make sure you sign up for the
guided tour of HMS Victory. As much as I love our own
USS Constitution, "Old Ironsides," there is simply no
comparison between the two sailing ships. HMS Victory
was a First-Rate Ship of the Line. She carried 104 guns
across multiple gun decks (nearly twice the guns on
USS Constitution) and her guns were, generally, much
larger and more powerful. The Ships of the Line were

the battleships of their day and carried a crew of around 850. I highly encourage you to read up on the ship before you start climbing around her. Besides seeing the place where Nelson was shot, you will also visit the spot in the interior where he finally passed on, his final words being "Thank God I have done my duty." Nelson had a brilliant naval career that epitomized the spirit of the famous patriotic song "Rule Britannia" whose lyrics begin "Rule Britannia, Britannia rule the waves."

While wandering around the historic dockyard, after the amazing visit to *HMS Victory*, I was incredibly fortunate to stumble upon a barely marked large hangar building where a tattered sail was hanging out for airing. It was the mainsail from *HMS Victory*, hanging from a yardarm within the building. The signage there stated that this was the first time since Trafalgar (in 1805) that the mainsail had been spread out. You could see the numerous tears from where cannon balls and chain shot ripped through it. I cannot begin to tell you what an incredible thrill that was.

In case the world's most spectacular sailing warship isn't your cup of tea, Portsmouth has much more to offer. I highly recommend the harbor tour by boat. You'll get to sail about an active British naval port and I can guarantee you'll be impressed by the modern aircraft carriers, destroyers, and an array of lesser ships that you'll encounter on the journey. My son loved the boat ride. I did, too.

After our harbor tour, we visited the *Mary Rose*

Museum where we got to see the remains of the 16th Century Tudor warship. Pre-dating *HMS Victory* by nearly 300 years, the *Mary Rose* was said to be Henry VIII's favorite ship. The Mary Rose sank in 1545 and only 35 of the 500 men onboard survived. The wreck of the Mary Rose was not discovered until 1971. What remained of the ship was raised on October 11, 1982. While the recovered section may not be aesthetically pleasing, the thousands of artifacts that were brought up represent an amazing time capsule of the period and the museum is filled with great exhibits and informative displays. If you love maritime history, you definitely won't be disappointed.

If you prefer to see a spectacular intact ship, go visit HMS Warrior. HMS Warrior, built in 1860, was the world's first iron-hulled, armored battleship. Powered by both steam and sail, she was the largest, fastest, and most powerful warship of her day. If you visited *HMS Victory* first, you'll truly be impressed by the incredible advances in technology that are apparent in every feature of this remarkable vessel. Its history isn't quite as storied as HMS Victory but you won't be disappointed as you climb around the ship. While there, definitely spend some time in the National Museum of the Royal Navy (called the Royal Navy Museum, when I visited).

If you are totally "shipped out," or if the little people are begging for mercy, you can do like we did and visit the Blue Reef Aquarium (called the Portsmouth Sealife

Centre, during my time visiting). The aquarium has a very nice collection of animals sure to entertain those who love fish, amphibians, reptiles, and especially cute sea otters.

There are a number of other really fun things to do while you're in Portsmouth and, of course, great places to eat. If you want, you can even take a ferry or, better yet, the hovercraft over to the Isle of Wight. I definitely encourage you to do some research before you travel so that you may tailor the experience for your travel party's tastes. With that said, if you're up for an immersion in maritime history, you'll find ample activities to fill your schedule.

While not something you visit, I would be remiss if I didn't conclude my discussion of touring Britain's maritime history without talking about the people. During my time in the United Kingdom, I had the honor of speaking with a number of World War II Royal Navy veterans. The stories they told were nothing short of remarkable. One elderly gentleman described how he was on a vessel which was torpedoed and sunk. And then he was transferred to another vessel, which was also torpedoed and sunk. I listened, in awe, to these marvelous story tellers. Whether speaking with fisherman, merchant sailors, or military veterans, you'll find countless men and women with amazing sea tales to share. You have but to ask…and perhaps offer to buy them a pint of their drink of choice. As I marched in the Southend-on-Sea annual Pearl Harbor Day Memorial

Parade, which included a wreath-laying ceremony and beautiful church service, I could not help but be inspired by the gratitude expressed by our British allies. After the day's formal activities, they always invited us over to their veteran's association building, a venue bedecked with all manner of nautical displays and trinkets. It was here that I heard some of the most compelling stories and I could not help but notice the pride in the eyes of the Royal Navy veterans who clearly felt an unbroken connection with centuries of British sailors. I was not surprised that one of the treasures of this meeting place was a beautiful wooden model of HMS Victory. Rule Britannia, Britannia rule the waves.

PHOTOS:

Cutty Sark, *14 Feb 1998*

David Lange and son straddling Prime Meridian, 14 Feb 1998

Royal Observatory, 14 Feb 1998

Royal Observatory, 14 Feb 1998

HMS Victory (Stern Gallery), 5 Sep 1998

David Lange and son standing in front of HMS
Victory, *5 Sep 1998*

Tattered mainsail from HMS Victory, *5 Sep 1998*

HMS Warrior, *6 Sep 1998*

Hiding Away in Camden

VANESSA CARAVEO

Let me disappear for a day
into the humming, buzzing crowds
of the bustling Camden Market,
fading facelessly upon a sidewalk's currents.

Give me just a sliver of space between people
with which to glimpse the storefronts,
colorful and customized and clumsy,
licking at the soul of my credit card.

Grant me a Sunday between food stalls,
with the sticky-sweet scent of grease,
entrenched in London's tourist traps
amidst all the foods of Camden.

Let me fill my bags to bursting
with trinkets and clothes and books.
Some twinkle, some smell, some wrinkle,
but everything belongs to me.

Abandon me in a niche shop
Maybe goth, maybe neon.
Let all of London know I'm hiding
amidst the pricey gifts of Camden.

Drop me off and let me wander,
where I'm meant to be.
lost in an ocean of souvenirs,
swimming upstream against the crowd,
on a lazy day

Give me a day when no one can find me,
not for work or for chores or for errands.
An old-fashioned shopping spree
amidst the flashy shops of Camden.

I only need the shelves, the streets,
the loud voices of vendors the shameless sprinklings of personality
in a public place,
lamplit lives all running in circles
in the dreamlike world of Camden

Harry Potter Experience
Riya Subbaiah

If you have been waiting for your Hogwarts letter
Just as long as I
Then ensure the Harry Potter Experience
Is not a sight you let pass by

Step into the Great Hall
A dining room whose magic captured us all
Race up the winding stairs to the Gryffyndor dorms
Where you can place yourself the common room
Where so many mysteries were solved

The Warner Brothers Studio truly comes to life
And awakens dreams of children and adults alike
Quidditch rules, costumes, and wigs line the walls
(Including Hermione's dress for the Yule Ball)
And when the day is through
Celebrate with a Butterbeer (or two)

The Lakes Court Hotel

LINDA TROTT DICKMAN

Carlisle, UK
for Moray Henderson

Here near the Queen's private entrance, we relaxed, exhaled.
We knew exactly how Victoria felt. That was no secret at all.
Imagine a hotel built for her maiden visit.

Our first time driving left, now hours late journeying from Stonehenge
to Carlisle.
We called ahead. Mum Henderson had the kitchen held open.
Just for us.
No menu item beyond our reach, a special wine, uncorked.
Aromas of roast duck, gnocchi with mushroom sauce beckoned.
Many attending to our needs.

Here within steps of a castle stormed by William Wallace,
close to a priory where King Edward the first recuperated.
Where a wee rabbit trifled with Mr. MacGregor's garden.
Here where the used book stores held tomes
older than our country. We were royally welcomed by friends
of another King, meeting for the first time.

LIFE'S LOTTERY

WENDY JONES NAKANISHI

The eighteenth-century English poet Alexander Pope believed it is our perverse fate never to be satisfied with our lot. We humans always anticipate a future happiness that is an improvement on any contentment we enjoy at present. We fail to appreciate our blessings, forever expecting tomorrow to be better. As Pope observed in his magnum opus *The Essay on Man*, 'Hope springs eternal in the human breast/Man never Is but always To be blest'.

I concur. As a student of human nature—and of Augustan literature—it is an observation I have often made myself, and often *of* myself. Still, I couldn't entirely suppress a surge of wild optimism as I boarded a British Airways flight at Kansai Airport bound for London in March 2020, nor banish the conviction that I was about to embark on the most joyous period of my life. I was finally going to live where I had always longed to live.

I considered England my spiritual homeland. A lover of books since I'd first learned to read, it was the setting of many of my favorite novels: the adventure stories of Robert Louis Stevenson, the romantic epics of the Bronte sisters, and the Sherlock Holmes mysteries. Above all, it was where Jane Austen's heroines fulfilled their destiny by meeting suitably conscious and conscientious suitors, with their marriage representing a union of equals in sense and sensibility.

As a child, I chafed against the fate that had led to my being born and raised in a rural outback in northern Indiana. I felt it was a cosmic mistake. As whatever deity ruled the heavens signally had failed me, it was up to me to rectify the error.

When I was offered a month-long trip to Europe through the auspices of the American Institute for Foreign Study as a high school graduation present, I naturally jumped at the chance, especially as one of the options included two weeks spent at the University of Southampton. I am pleased to report that England did not disappoint. It was the early seventies, and men in London still wore formal suits and bowler hats and carried black furled umbrellas. The incessant rain conferred a misty charm to the wealth of palaces and churches and monuments, to magnificent squares of elegant houses, to cobbled streets dividing rows of

Victorian terraces, to huge parks with impossibly green grass and rivers thronged with swans and ducks.

In my stay at Southampton, some friendly British students took a group of us to a pub and I had my first taste of mead—and of the heady excitement of pub culture. At the university, we had lectures on the Neolithic stone circles and Anglo-Saxon burial mounds common in the area. We occasionally took excursions into the countryside to see some examples of the 'barrows' or richly furnished wooden rooms within the mounds constructed for royalty and prominent members of the aristocracy over a thousand years before. Coming from a town in the Midwest founded in the 1860s, it was thrilling to contemplate a history stretching back through the mists of time.

The AIFS itinerary I had chosen also included a quick tour of European capitals—Paris, Zurich, Vienna, Rome—followed by a two-week Mediterranean cruise. But I found it hard to summon up enthusiasm. My love affair with Britain was in its first full flush and I didn't want to leave it.

Still, I soon managed to return. As a student at Indiana University, I arranged to join a 'Junior Year Abroad' program at Lancaster University in northwest England, one of several new universities founded in the 1960s. Of course, I'd have preferred the dreaming spires of Oxford, and I admit to disappointment when I first arrived and was confronted by brutalist architecture and windy squares. But I became accustomed and gradually learned to love the campus's stark functionality.

It's a commonplace that people in the north of England are friendlier than those in the south. Certainly, I was given a warm welcome once I got to know classmates and fellow residents of my dormitory. I was the little Yank they liked to patronize and instruct. They laughingly taught me how to order beer at a pub, how to make a proper cup of tea, how to relish fish and chips and steak-and-kidney pudding, and, on our long walks through the countryside, how to appreciate the bleak beauty of Lancashire, with its forests and dales, moors, and mountains.

I learned to love Lancaster sufficiently that I returned to do an MA at the university a few years later. When, in the mid-nineties, I was offered a year's sabbatical by my university in southern Japan, I didn't think twice where I wanted to spend it, even though I had also lived in Edinburgh for four years in the early eighties, getting a doctorate on Pope's letters. Edinburgh was charming; Lancaster was home. I felt this so deeply that I ended up purchasing a small house near Lancaster castle in the late nineties, renting it out while I was still working in Japan.

I finally took possession of my little Victorian terraced house in the spring of 2020 on retiring after thirty-six years of full-time employment as an English professor at a Japanese university. The timing was unfortunate. I arrived in the UK three days after it entered its first lockdown. I landed at Heathrow and was dismayed to find the bustling airport I knew reduced to a shadow of its former self. There were few people about, not even immigration officials. We passengers needed to scan our passports in machines. In the eerie silence that reigned, we scurried almost furtively to the baggage claim area to collect our suitcases, guiltily avoiding each other's gaze as if we had committed a kind of sin simply by being out and about.

I took the Paddington Express and then a taxi to Euston, where I could catch a train to Lancaster. Whirling down deserted city streets lined by shops and offices and pubs, all closed, was another dispiriting experience. I scarcely saw a soul. I felt I'd been transported to some alternate universe in which mankind had abruptly been wiped out by a mysterious disease (which, in a sense, was true), leaving the artifacts of human civilization standing untended and empty.

I arrived at Lancaster station at about eight in the evening, about thirty-five hours after I'd set off from my home in Japan. The nightmare continued. Lancaster also had dwindled into a dystopian version of itself. Used to seeing a lively town center crowded with strollers, shoppers, and revelers, the shops, pubs, and restaurants thronged, it was an unpleasant shock to find myself virtually alone. With a heavy heart, I wheeled my heavy suitcases down dark cobbled streets wet with rain, bound for the private hotel I had booked for two weeks, intending to spend a period of self-isolation there.

When my quarantine was up and I finally allowed myself to enter my own house, I was dismayed by the realization that it was empty, holding only a few stained carpets and torn curtains left by the previous tenants. Only the loft was full, but it was filled with things tenants had wanted to get rid of—old television sets, broken down heaters, rolls of cloth, even some artificial trees. There were also the few pieces I had stored there —goods I had used during my sabbatical year—but they were inadequate for my needs, including only one table, four hardback chairs, a dismantled bed, some crockery, and two sleeping bags. I wondered if I'd be reduced to camping out in the front room beside its beautiful old tiled Victorian fireplace.

I was seized by a sense of desperation. I had two tasks to accomplish. First, I needed somehow to furnish and equip my home. Second, I wanted to empty the loft of all its rubbish. But I wondered how I might do this during lockdown. Grocery stores and those offering what were deemed essential items were open; all others were closed. On searching online for furniture that I could order and that would be delivered to my house, I realized I needed, finally, to buy a mobile phone, as I'd not be allowed to purchase anything without one. In Japan my husband and I had been proud of our status as modern Luddites, refusing to buy phones because we valued our personal privacy so highly. I needed to ditch this principle to survive. Crucially, I obtained the services of a handyman willing to bend the law and enter my home. It was a win-win situation for us both. He needed the work; I desperately needed assistance. He put up curtains, repaired broken skirting boards, assembled furniture delivered in flat packs, painted walls, took unwanted items to the city dump, and even brought in a professional vacuum cleaner that made some inroads on the stains in the carpets. After some three or four months, with his help, I managed to get my home in habitable order.

Once that huge task was accomplished, I set about making a life for myself in my new home. I love Japan but living there—in the rural area where I've made my home—has always felt like a kind of exile to me. There are few fellow foreigners; I'm still stared at; hardly anyone speaks English. On moving to the UK, I wanted to make up for lost time, to engage in social activities inaccessible to me in Japan because of work and domestic responsibilities but also because, often, they simply weren't on offer. Once my house was livable, I joined a choir, a speech club, and a bowling club. I became a volunteer at a nature reserve and a local cinema/theatre. I arranged weekly long walks and cycle rides with friends.

I am now on my eighth—but not consecutive—year of residence in the UK. Familiarity has not bred contempt. I agree with Cecil Rhodes that to be born British is to win first prize in the lottery of life. I believe it to be the most civilized country on earth—the most tolerant, the most generous, the most principled.

It is the oldest democracy on earth—governed by the rule of law—and was one of the first nations in the world to abolish slavery and actively try to prevent it by intercepting and turning back slave ships at sea. Its National Health Service, founded after the second world war, is, however flawed, an idealistic attempt to make free medical care available to all its citizens. Its media— newspapers, radio, and television—is excellent, often of the highest standard imaginable. Alas, in recent years, Britain has been beating itself up about its colonial past, but I think it fails to recall all the advantages it conferred on the countries it once governed, many of which still depend on the infrastructure built during British rule or who fondly remember a government which at least professed principles of fairness and justice and seemed to seek to implement them.

In my daily life in the UK, I count my blessings. I can walk to the beautiful Lancaster city center each morning to buy a good newspaper and, once back home, read it while listening to Radio Three, with its wonderful programs featuring not only classical music and opera but also jazz and world music as well as presentations on the arts.

The food I can buy—either at a restaurant or in a grocery—is of a standard far higher, and of a variety far greater than what was available when I first lived in the UK in the mid-seventies. Then, as a spoiled American teenager, accustomed to being able to buy nearly anything I wanted, I'd been astonished and dismayed by the limited selection of goods available in the shops. Now, there is an abundance of good fresh fruit and vegetables and ethnic ingredients.

Similarly, while I'd shivered through my first years in the UK because the houses I inhabited were warmed only by coal fires or by heaters with a few electric bars, central heating has become common in Britain. But it's still a relatively recent phenomenon. I recall getting chilblains during my time in Edinburgh–and not knowing what they were until I consulted a doctor. Similarly, my legs developed what another Scottish doctor laughingly called 'lazy tartan': mottled skin caused by sitting too close to a fire.

It would be hard to pinpoint what I love most about the UK, but I can make a list. I love the British sense of humor: their self-deprecation, their irony and ready wit. I love British pubs, with their warm, welcoming atmosphere and the sense they give of a peculiarly national tradition of fondness for drink and conversation. I love the British countryside for its beauty, for the great variety of scenery from north to south, from east to west, and for the fact that it is widely accessible through a huge network of well-maintained public footpaths and cycleways. As an American accustomed to ugly urban sprawl in the States, whenever I travel by train in Britain, I marvel at how much land remains preserved as green fields bounded by hedges or as forests and meadows. I love the British disposition, which I'd characterize as one based on notions of kindness and fair play. There is not only a tolerance of eccentricity but also a fondness for it. I admire Britons' irreverence and their willingness to flout laws they believe unreasonable. This was especially apparent during Covid. I love Japan, but the Japanese sometimes strike me as too conformist, too obedient.

I even love the UK's notoriously horrible weather! Some British friends I've made who have become long-term ex-pats often cite the climate as a reason for their self-imposed exile. But I find it exciting in its changeableness, its infinite variety. In some places, at certain times, we can experience all four seasons in a single day: the heat of summer, autumn's brisk winds, winter's chill, and spring rains.

Common wisdom says life is what we make of it. I'm glad mine has included a chance to spend time in a country I love, and that my own decisions, along with fate, have brought me my heart's desire. I know myself to be blessed.

MEET OUR CONTRIBUTORS

Donna Keel Armer is the author of Solo in Salento: A Memoir which has now been translated into Italian as Un'americana in Salento. Psychology and Social Sciences were her undergraduate studies at Mississippi University for Women with her graduate studies in theology. She is a docent at the Pat Conroy Literary Center, a member of SAGE, a volunteer at Hunting Island State Park and a past board member of Friends of the Library. She is a world traveler, enthusiastic lover of food and wine, and has numerous articles published in local South Carolina magazines. A native of Richmond, Virginia, she now resides in Beaufort, South Carolina with her husband of forty years where she is working on a suspense series set between the Lowcountry and Italy.

Katrenia G. Busch is a producer for a local CBS TV news station. She is the author of Contesting the Conscience: an Interview with the Ego, an essay on psychoanalysis. She authored the award-winning poem, "Mystery and Wind" chosen by League of Innovation (2022). Her works have appeared in Police Writers, Flora Fiction, 50 Give or Take amongst others.

Vanessa Caraveo is an award-winning bilingual author, published poet, and artist who has a passion for promoting inclusion, empowerment and equality for all, helping others discover the power they possess within themselves to overcome adversity and reach their fullest potential. She is involved with various organizations that assist children and adults with disabilities and enjoys working with non-profit groups and volunteering in the promotion of literacy. Vanessa aspires to continue making a positive difference in many lives through her service to others and literary work.

Kathryn Cockrill is an author, writer and poet based in the UK. Her first book was published in 2018, a collection of short stories entitled Case Files of the Supernatural. When her head isn't buried in a book,

Kathryn can be found drinking bubble tea, walking with her two dogs or living out her heroine protagonist dreams by training in horseback archery and knife throwing.

Debbie De Louise is an award-winning author and a reference librarian at a public library on Long Island. She is a member of Sisters-in-Crime, International Thriller Writers, the Long Island Authors Group, and the Cat Writers' Association. She writes two cozy mystery series, the Cobble Cove Mysteries and the new Buttercup Bend Mysteries. She's also written a paranormal romance, three standalone mysteries, a time-travel novel, and a collection of cat poems. Debbie has also contributed to several Red Penguin Collection anthologies and their Bloom Literary Journal. She also writes for Catster Magazine. Debbie lives on Long Island with her husband, daughter, and two cats. You can learn more about her and writing by visiting her website at https://debbiedelouise.com where you can subscribe to her blog and/or newsletter.

While working as an IT professional, usually as a project manager, Steve deWolfe has been composing poetry on such subjects as life, love, and sports, sometimes with an unusual point of view. His "Final Flight - A Baseball's Story", from the point of view of the baseball, was accepted by the National Baseball Hall of Fame. Other works appear in several Red Penguin anthologies. His business travels have taken him to several cities, and he now welcomes the opportunity to share his memories of some of them with Red Penguin Collection readers. As a husband, father, and grandfather, Steve was born in Brooklyn, NY, spent decades in New Jersey, and now enjoys the working and the weather in Jacksonville, Florida.

Linda Trott Dickman—an award winning poet, author of four chapbooks, and a poetry prompt book for children. Her work has been featured in local, international and online anthologies. She is the coordinator of poetry for the Northport Arts Coalition. She teaches at the Walt Whitman Birthplace, the local Historical Society and leads a poetry workshop at Samantha's Li'l Bit O' Heaven coffee house. Linda is a consultant for Penn. State University in the Global Teach Agriculture and Literature Program under Dr. Hiram Larew.

Dany Gagnon is an artist, game publisher, translator, and writer living in Montréal, Canada. In the last two years, her poetry has appeared in over a dozen publications. She was awarded Second Prize for the Polar Expression Poetry Contest 2021. Her writing explores the bond between words, memories, and emotions.

Elaine Gilmartin is a therapist by profession, which is actually a great career for writers because she gets into people's heads and hears stories that can seem too fantastic even for fiction. It's also helpful in that it is her job to challenge how they perceive themselves and the world around them, not always an easy task! Elaine has written a number of articles for the online site Medium and has self-published a non-fiction book on handling the emotional struggles many faced during the pandemic. She is a member of Women's Fiction Writers and Long Island Authors and had a short story featured on a January podcast called, Horrorific.

Noelle Grassel's passion for creative writing started from a young age and blossomed during her time at SUNY New Paltz, where she studied it to perfect her craft. She is 25 years old from Long Island, New York and loves all things travel, dogs, and Harry Styles. If she isn't spending time with her friends and family, you can almost always find her around her sweet German Shepherd, Schatzi.

Nusrat Haider is currently working in the nursing field in Accident and Emergency Dept. She Likes to doodle with words in her free time and enjoys reading fiction and poetry. Writing is therapy to NUsrat. Nusrat has been published in the following anthologies: Black Lives Matter, Leicester 2084AD, Wondering Souls, Bollocks to Brexit and Settled Status in the UK to name but a few, and is absolutely delighted to contribute to this upcoming anthology.

Mark Andrew Heathcote is adult learning difficulties support worker. He has poems published in journals, magazines, and anthologies both online and in print. He resides in the UK, and is from Manchester. Mark is the author of "In Perpetuity" and "Back on Earth," two books of poems published by Creative Talents Unleashed.

David Lange was born and grew up on Long Island, New York. A graduate of the United States Air Force Academy, he served for 30 years as an Active Duty officer in the United States Air Force before retiring in 2018. Colonel Lange is a decorated combat veteran and flew numerous combat, combat support, and humanitarian relief missions during his career. He was awarded the prestigious Institute of Navigation Superior Achievement Award in recognition of his life-long accomplishments as a practicing navigator. David loves sharing stories of hope and inspiration. He has numerous short stories, essays, and poems published within various anthologies and his memoir, "Quest: My Journey Through La Mancha," was published in 2020.

Matt McGee writes in the Los Angeles area. In 2022 his work has appeared in Gypsum Tales, Sweetycat Press and Red Penguin. When not typing he drives around in rented cars and plays goalie in local hockey leagues.

Rex McGregor is a New Zealand playwright. His short comedies have been produced on four continents from New York and London to Sydney and Chennai. https://www.rexmcgregor.com/

Wendy Jones Nakanishi, an American by birth, has spent most of her life abroad, including six months in Holland, a year in Paris, eight in the UK, and thirty-six in Japan where, married to a Japanese farmer, she worked full-time at a private university on the island of Shikoku, retiring in the spring of 2022. In addition to research related to her PhD on Alexander Pope (Edinburgh, 1984) she has published widely on Japanese and British literature and, under the pen name of Lea O'Harra, is the author of three crime fiction novels set in rural modern-day Japan: 'Imperfect Strangers' (2015); 'Progeny' (2016); and 'Lady First' (2017). 'Dead Reckoning', a murder mystery set in the American Midwest, is due to be published soon by Sharpe Books.

Donna Norman-Carbone has a passion for writing women's fiction that tugs at the heartstrings. She is the author of two upcoming women's fiction novels, All That is Sacred (2023) and Of Lies and Honey (2024) published by Red Adept Publishing. After having taught as a university adjunct and adult educator, Donna currently teaches writing, film and British literature to high school students. She lives in a small Connecticut suburb where she and her husband have raised three wonderful and creative children, two Labrador Retrievers and a Siamese cat.

Donna holds a master's degree in English from Southern CT State University, she is a member of the Women's Fiction Writers Association and a tour guide for the Bookish Road Trip. In her spare time, Donna enjoys reading a good book on a sunny Cape Cod beach, traveling worldwide to immerse herself in other cultures, and spending cherished time with family and friends.

Carol Orange has worked in the art world for more than twenty years. She began as a research editor on art books in London and later became an art dealer in Boston. She has an MBA from Simmons University and worked as a marketing manager at the Polaroid Corporation. Along with concert pianist Virginia Eskin who played Chopin's music, she read excerpts from George Sand's novels in three salons at the French Library in Boston. Her debut novel A DISCERNING EYE was inspired by the world's largest unsolved theft at Boston's Isabella Stewart Gardner Museum. Her protagonist, Portia Malatesta, is a Boston art dealer. She analyzes the thirteen stolen art works and discovers an underlying theme of tension between light and dark. A DISCERNING EYE won the Global Book Award for mystery/suspense.

Valerie Ormond retired as a Navy Captain after a twenty-five-year career as a U.S. Naval intelligence officer and began her second career as a writer. Valerie's first two novels, "Believing In Horses," and "Believing In Horses, Too," won eight national and international awards. Her most recent novel, "Believing In Horses Out West," won first place in the National Federation of Press Women's (NFPW's) national 2022 Communications Contest; second place in the 2022 BookFest™ Awards; was a finalist in the 2021 Wishing Shelf Book Awards, and is currently a finalist in the 2022 Military Writers Society of America book awards program. Red Penguin Books published her short story "Be Brave" in "Ernest Lived and Other Historical Fiction Stories." This story of a Pony Express rider won first place in NFPW's 2022 at-large communications contest and third place at the national level. Valerie's fiction and non-fiction stories, poems, and articles have appeared internationally in books, magazines, newspapers, and blogs.

Amber Primdahl is a photographer with a love for travel. She also creates content on well-being, style, manifestation, and living a cozy life on her YouTube and social media accounts (amber.noamedia).

William John Rostron is the author of a series of novels steeped in the music and culture in the late 20th and early 21st centuries. Band in the Wind, Sound of Redemption, and Brotherhood of Forever have received critical acclaim from Writers Digest, the Online Book Club Review, and many other reviewers. These books have found readership on four continents (North America, Europe, Australia, and Asia). He has been published in fifteen Red Penguin anthologies and four Visible Ink anthologies. The Visible Ink pieces have been produced for the New York stage and are available for viewing at WilliamJohnRostron.com. An anthology of short pieces entitled A Flamingo Under the Carousel has recently been published by Red Penguin Books.

Born and raised in Queens, NY, William John Rostron now splits his time between his home on Eastern Long Island and traveling the country in his Tiffin motorhome. When not writing, he is busy completing a bucket list of travel adventures. In the past 17 years, he and his wife Marilyn have traveled 140,000 miles. These journeys have taken them to the 48 contiguous states, 133 national parks, all 30 major league baseball stadiums, 154 cities and towns, two Canadian provinces, and a variety of unusual experiences and locations. Many of these locations have served as backgrounds for his books.

He is working on a fourth novel, Lost in the Wind, and a second book of short stories.

www.WilliamJohnRostron.com

Annette Towler was born in England and moved to the United States in the early 1990s. She enjoys art job as a therapist, and in her spare time likes to run. Annette has a sweet cat called Marsha.

Janet Metz Walter grew up in Queens NY. She realized very early in life that she wanted to write, and throughout her careers in various social service agencies she wrote local newsletters and professional articles. She also wrote and produced shows in camps and community theater productions. She has been a travel agent, world traveler and teacher in Adult Continuing Ed in several schools, and has taught classes in the game of Mah Jongg for 18 years.

In 2009 she joined her husband in his fine jewelry business, Gold Fire Diamonds as Vice President in charge of the website and marketing. She realized her lifelong dream when she wrote her book "The 2 Carrot Ring and Other Fascinating Jewelry Stories," a collection of people's personal stories about their pieces of jewelry.

She also is available for interactive group programs about the book.

Janet has also contributed to the Red Penguin anthologies "Realiteen:Reflections on Growing Up," "Feeding The Flock:Recipes From the Red Penguin Family" and "Finding Family."

janetwalter.bsl@gmail.com

www.goldfirediamonds.com

CPSIA information can be obtained
at www.ICGtesting.com
Printed in the USA
LVHW021452181122
733280LV00004B/193